the corset maker

Volume One

K.T. FREDERICK

This book is a work of fiction. Names, characters, places, and incidents are either the product of the author's imagination or are used fictitiously. Any resemblance to actual persons, living or dead, events or locals is entirely coincidental.

The Corset Maker, Volume One
First Edition: November 2015
ISBN: 978-0-9949307-2-9

If you're going through hell, keep on going.

— Winston Churchill

acknowledgments

With tremendous thanks to all my writing partners, beta readers, poetry advisors, and supporters who believed I could bring this story to life.

Special thanks to my parents. Daddy you still aren't allowed to read this and Mom, don't worry, I'll keep believing. To my big sister Keewa, also Judi Pattison—my copy editor, as well as writing partners Shauna Clinning and Joanne Yordanou, To Vicky Hepworth, Giedra Poska, Thelma & Louise and Brian Henry with his merry band of writers—thank you and each of you know why.

Sincerest gratitude to Danielle Maitt for book cover and design and Tiffany Turpin Johnson who taught me about the "beats"—we always need the beats. To Nitin Page for being my poetry confidant. For reminding me that the honest emotions are gifts we give to ourselves and the reader.

And with deepest appreciation to Troy, for believing I can do anything and making that SOP in our home for the last fourteen years. This wouldn't have been possible without your undying belief in people's potential. My sincerest love and thanks to you.

chapter one

"TIME!" I YELL. "WHAT'S THE TIME?"

By now I'm airborne, shoving burnt toast in my mouth as I load my shoulders with straps. Last night's epic thunderstorm knocked out the electricity to 10,000 homes in the Lower East Side, including ours. No electricity means my dead cell phone wasn't charged, and therefore no alarm clock.

You'd think by 9:20 a.m., any self-respecting 21-year-olds trying to make a career in New York City would be awake, and normally we would be. But we've got things going on. Big things that have required late-night investments of time. Like preparing for our big pitch to movie director, producer, author, and poet-extraordinaire Julien Wolfe on Monday. Like packing for tonight's film festival. Like creeping on Julien Wolfe's poetry webpage.

"What's the time, Chlo?" I ask again.

"Late! The time is late!" Chloe says, as the door slams behind us and we beat feet down our triplex's front steps. The numerous bags hanging from our bodies bounce with every footfall. We need to catch the J-line and then the bus. The subway is no problem. The driver of the bus — Crusty, we like to call him — hates waiting, and we're always running late. In fact, he loves the looks on our faces when we've missed his closing doors by nanoseconds.

As predicted, the subway's packed with students and recent grads like us. For those not heading to work, the destination is NYU or Columbia or some vocational school for the arts. The minute we step off, we run toward our bus stop. Crusty's there now, and by the look on his face, he's already held the doors open for 30 seconds. Our feet slow, slapping the pavement just as he's closing the doors. I slide my hand between the pinching glass panes. Crusty sneers as we pant and ascend the steps to make our fare. *Not this time, bucko, not this time.*

The bus is packed and Chloe takes a seat along the back row. I find my own spot halfway down on the right. When I sit, I land hard with a gust of breath and before I can relax, my hands quickly scramble to check that I have everything with me. Backpack with loathsome uniform? Check. Evening gown for tonight's film festival after shift at loathsome job? Check. Tickets for tonight's event, given to me by exhausting mother? Check.

My arms ache from running with too many bags, and I'm glistening with sweat. It's your typical September in Manhattan, and the pavement still smokes from the heat of the sun. A placard resting against the bus's windshield says the A/C is broken. *Great*.

This jalopy is always filled with the same eclectic passengers. "Sweaty Eddie," a ginger-bearded, young hipster who knits his own sweaters and insists on wearing them to class no matter the temperature, has decided to stand in front of me. He's just raised his arm to hang on to the ceiling's handrail, and I think I'm going to die. The fumes he gives off waft in my direction. My watering eyes flick to Chloe. She meets my gaze with a mischievous grin and pinches her nose.

Her seat isn't much better. Beside her is the wannabe Kardashian OMG'ing into her pink bedazzled phone, and I know my best friend would give anything to be sitting somewhere else. I raise my hand and shape it like a duck's bill to give her the "clacking hand," and we both burst out laughing.

Since my phone is sitting at the bottom of my purse with a portable charge attached to it, I check my wristwatch: 9:45 a.m. Still four more stops until we sprint to work. It's near Broadway and Tribeca, home of the theater district—my Mecca. There, the energy is electric: a mix of small and large theaters, museums and major television studios. Sadly, I don't work in any of those buildings, but rather at The Hen in the Cock House, a Hooters-esque pub located on the edge of the Financial District and filled with young, handsy bankers. They grope and they're gross, but they tip like mofos. And despite my slapping their hands away, they tip enough for Chloe and me to afford our small apartment and build our costume-making company. *Amulet Designs* is the dream we've held since the day we graduated from the Theatrical Institute of Design. We want to—I mean, we *will*—land some of the most prestigious movie contracts and design some of the most ornate costumes for the film industry.

I affectionately pat my laptop bag at the goldmine resting inside. The photo proofs on my hard drive are our one-way ticket out of waitressing hell, where our barely-covered boobs are part of the uniform. When we aren't waitressing, we're designing corsets and other small theater costumes, or I'm blogging and tweeting about design and surfing Julien Wolfe's website. Not only am I a seamstress, I'm also co-owner and spokesperson for our company.

My gaze drifts to the bagged evening gown, also resting in my lap, pressed and dry-cleaned for this evening. It's long and sleek and the color of green olives. My copper red hair currently sits high in a long ponytail for work, but later it will fall long and wavy and in contrast with my dress.

Chloe mouths the word "tickets." I pat my purse

and give her a wink. She sits back in her seat with a slump of relief.

My mother, Claudia Worthington, is a world-renowned costume designer living in L.A. She's currently in Scotland on location for an epic TV series. She's the one who slipped us the tickets for tonight's movie premiere. A premiere Julien Wolfe directed.

He's a 29-year-old savant with a camera.

Tonight, his film, *Not My Father's Hands,* is debuting. A low-budget flick he wrote, produced and directed that's already awash with Oscar buzz.

I pick up a commuter newspaper wedged between my seat and the one next to me. Gracing the cover is a picture of Julien. He was out on the town last night, dressed in a short black leather jacket, white t-shirt, and low-hung faded jeans. He's matured since his late teens. Back then he was in and out of trouble with the law. But not anymore. Not in the last five years anyway. I'm vibrating with excitement knowing he's in the same city as me. Me and the other 8.4 million people. Either way, I'm going to see him tonight and again on Monday, and the thought fills me with anticipation.

"He rocks," Sweaty says, hovering over me, admiring the shot of my teenage crush.

Being near Eddie's odor is suddenly bearable. "I'm going to see his movie tonight at the film festival," I tell him.

"Oh! That's the one about his dad, isn't it? That

movie's supposed to tell us the truth about what really happened to Julien's mom, right?"

"I think so," I say, though I'm not entirely sure. "I get the impression no one knows what happened to her."

Sweaty has already turned away and is reading his phone. Seems he's not as interested in the truth as he'd like me to believe.

Julien's the son of the late film director Richard Wolfe. I've heard tonight's showing is a recount about the troubled life his father lived and how his fall from grace came after the mysterious death of his wife, Julien's mother. A fall that eventually led to his father's own death and Julien's troubles with the law. I don't think anyone knows who killed Julien's mother. The police never found her murderer. I keep that to myself.

I'm surprised Sweaty Eddie knows anything about the Richard Wolfe scandal. Sweaty is younger than me by at least three years, and I was only thirteen when I learned about the court-case. L.A. was abuzz, and Julien was on the cover of countless teen magazines. He always looked exhausted. Mom said she thought it was disgusting the way the media used the court case to sell magazines. Richard Wolfe was charged, but later acquitted. He was never the same after his wife's death, and only Julien knows what the man went through.

Everyone wants to see this film.

One stop before ours I'm assaulted by a new

wave of fumes. Eddie's pits are now mixed with someone's greasy breakfast sandwich. I remind myself it doesn't matter and pat my laptop bag again. In here lies my ticket to freedom. All our vintage corset designs and modeling photos sit safely on my hard drive, while the costumes themselves sit in storage, back at our place. Over the past month, we've spent our waitressing tips on hiring models and struck a deal with a photographer friend of ours. All this for Monday's big pitch to Julien's production team for his upcoming time travel film.

"That's not your seat!" someone yells at the front of the bus. There's more shouting, then a wave of falling people and a crush of toppling bodies. It's a fight for the third time this week, and Sweaty Eddie's now on top of me. I think I'm going to die, not just from the impact, but from the smell. I struggle to see Chloe, but she's nowhere.

A fist meeting someone's jaw makes an audible crunch, but I can't see beyond the tangle of bodies trying to right themselves. It's now 10:25 a.m. Our shift starts at 10:30. We can't afford to be late—our boss will dock our pay. Even when we get off at the stop, we still need to run another 200 yards to The Hen.

We're parked at a red light, and our bus is sardined among a throng of cars. We aren't going anywhere anytime soon.

Crusty flings open the front doors and tosses out bodies. This makes more room on the car, giving people a chance to regain their footing. Finally I meet Chloe's gaze.

Run for it, she mouths, and pulls the cord. I grab my bags and meet her at the side exit. We run, zigzagging through the parked cars, and jog a few more yards before the traffic lifts and crawls forward. Crusty's bus passes us, and halts at another stop light just ahead.

Then I feel it.

The bags draping from my arms, they're too light. My heart races at the idea I may have forgotten something.

My laptop bag. Good god…my files.

I make a break and dart back between the parked cars waiting at the light. I pound on Crusty's doors. He's inside, but he won't look my way. His face is ruddy, and his hair and clothes are disheveled from the fight he's just broken up. My palm bangs on the glass of the door, and he still won't look at me. He just stares straight ahead, like he hates his life and wants everyone else to suffer along with him.

"Oh dear god, you have to open," I plead. "I forgot something!"

But he ignores me, and my hand is stinging from repeated blows against his glass doors. Chloe catches up, panting, and she, too, starts pounding and yelling.

The light turns green, and Crusty finally looks up and gives us a vengeful sneer just before he jams on the gas and takes off.

chapter two

COLOSSAL FAIL.

Everything hurts. I watch the bus growing smaller in the distance.

Chloe's eyes are frantic, just like my life this very moment.

"Your laptop?" Her voice is shrill.

How do I explain to my partner the magnitude of what's just happened? She's been relying on me to help get us out of student debt, keep us both fed, and pay the rent, which is already two weeks late. Landing Julien's account was our Hail Mary, and I'm watching it drive away on that bus.

"Yes, the laptop," I say, pushing my hand through my hair and fisting it into a bird's nest. I roll my lips inward in an effort to stifle the expletives that want to fly from my mouth.

"Oh, geez," she says, still staring at the bus that I can't bear to look at. "Does this mean all—"

"All of our photos for next week's pitch are on that bus," I finish. We were going to use my laptop and projector to present the corset photos to Julien's committee. We hadn't printed the proofs because our presentation was to be projected from our computer and displayed on a screen.

"It's okay, Amelia, you backed up all your files," Chloe reminds me, her voice calm. "I remember, you specifically told me you ran out of cloud storage and couldn't afford to buy more. So you backed them up on the flash drive instead. No problem."

She smiles.

My stomach churns. "I backed up the photos on two flash drives. Which are both in the front pocket of my laptop bag. Driving away."

Chloe's stunned gaze follows mine as we watch beady red lights turn left and out of sight.

"Oh shit," she says.

And shit is right.

"Do you think your mom could lend you some money to take some new photos?"

It's a fair question, considering my mother is wealthy, works in the same industry, and knows what it's like to make her wage from rags.

"No, she won't help me."

"I hate that about your mom," she says, her voice curt.

My best friend never speaks to me this way. I get why she's frustrated. This is my fault, but an argument about the merits of my mother's moral standards is not something I want to get into. Besides, it seems a little unfair, since her dad wouldn't fund us either, for different reasons.

Chloe's dad raised her by himself on a menial wage and would give her every last cent if he could. The man's a welder and lives in Yonkers. He's never been in a position to help Chloe financially. My mom's in a financial position to help — she just refuses. For mom, learning to make my way without her financial help teaches me to be resourceful. *Thank. You. Mother.*

"Grab your phone, Amelia, let's call the Transit Authority. They can get a message to Crusty."

I snag my phone from the bottom of my purse and hit the ON button. It has been charging since I left the house and has just enough power to make a call or two. Directory Assistance puts me through to Transit operations.

My face drops.

"What now?" Chloe says.

"I have to leave a message on their hotline. There's no one there to take my call."

I leave a message, hoping someone will contact Crusty while he's on the road. They'll have to call me at The Hen since we aren't allowed to carry our phones on the job, so now all I have to do is wait for the news that they found my bag.

Or my life's over.

We're 10 minutes late by the time we arrive at our joyous place of employment. Too numb to care at the scowl on our boss's face, we enter to a buzz of repairmen.

"What's going on?" I ask another waitress.

"The cash registers are down. Went offline because of last night's thunderstorm."

I'm relieved. Our boss has bigger problems than Chloe and me arriving 10 minutes late.

Chloe doesn't seem to notice, though. Her head is down. She's worried. And it's all my fault.

"Hey, if the Transit Authority can't find my laptop bag, I'll just call Jared."

Jared's our friend from university and the low-budget photographer we hired. He's also trying to make his way into a career, but in the fashion industry.

"He'll have the digital copies of the photos from our shoot. While I'm at it, I'll ask if he can let us borrow one of his laptops."

It's like she doesn't hear me. I touch her forearm, and she finally looks up.

"I'll make this right, Chloe. Don't lose faith in me." A slow smile creeps across her face, and I know she's finally heard me. I'm slightly relieved, and slightly petrified.

After the lunch crowd has been served, I dump a mitt-full of bankers' business cards into the garbage, remove my apron, and park myself in the back for my break.

The phone rings, and I race to the wall. "Cock in the Hen House! I mean, Hen in the Cock House!"

It's the Transit Authority.

After a few moments of corporate pleasantries and apologies, my shoulders slump. They don't have the laptop bag. Crusty is saying he hasn't seen it. I'm not sure if I believe that. I'm not sure it's going to matter. A missing laptop is a missing laptop, no matter who has it.

"All right, will you call me if someone happens to turn it in?" The rep agrees, and I finish up by giving my cell number.

I feel hollow, like an absolute failure. Jared has to have the digital copies. It's the only thing that will save us now.

Without my equipment, I can't blog on my own site. I'm truly embarrassed about my urge to check Julien's webpage, but what I'm jonesing for is a shot of his poetry. It's like heroin to me, and I need my daily fix. It's raw and mesmerizing. All of it adds to the mystique of the artistic director.

Julien posts a new poem daily, and I'm ashamed to admit I'm disappointed at missing today's installment. It's not like the post is going to leave his site. It's just that Julien's become my obsession. The man is an artist with skeletons. His photography always involves pictures of his hands, never his face. When it comes to media interviews, he never answers questions about his personal life, only his movies. He's moody and snaps at interviewers. He's a recluse. A buried rock. What I wouldn't give to unearth such a man.

I push thoughts of him from my mind. Lusting over the director isn't going to help my cause. I read his poetry until my phone died last night, and if I hadn't been in such a rush this morning, I could have avoided the catastrophe I'm in right now. I need to focus. Less Julien, more on the problem at hand. I wash my hands, as if to wash Julien from my mind.

Chloe pokes her head into the small area, scraping a plate into the hidden trashcan behind the wall. "Any luck with the Transit Authority?"

I had been waiting for her question, and I raise my head but don't meet her eyes. "They didn't find it. The laptop or the bag." I would bet money Crusty stole it just to spite me, but I could never prove it. I finish drying my hands and wave them like it's no big deal. "I left Jared a message," I tell her. He'll help us.

Chloe mouths *oh,* and heads back to the dining room, but not before I see the flash of worry across her face. She has every right to be concerned. If we don't land this deal with Julien's production, we won't get the advance to pay our overdue bills.

chapter three

BY 5 O'CLOCK, THE NIGHT IS BRIGHT, MUGGY, AND
still. The inner city's air hangs with the scent of
gasoline and hotdog stands. In preparation for the
film festival, we shower and change at The Hen.
The humidity gives my red tresses the bounce they
need. I smooth my hands down my ribcage. The
olive green dress Chloe took in for me hugs my
curves just right. The joy over tonight's premiere is
the only thing shadowing my excitement as I wait
for Jared to call me with good news.

We wait outside The Hen for the trendy cab we
e-hailed.

"Tips were strong today." Chloe's voice is more
upbeat than it was midday, and I'm relieved. Can't
have her losing faith in the captain of this ship. A
hybrid-taxi pulls up, and we jump in, thankful we
don't need to walk through town in heels.

"Still nothing from Jared?" Chloe asks again,

just as our driver breaks hard for a jaywalker.

"Not yet. He's probably busy with a shoot, I'm sure he'll check his messages tonight." He'd better. Jared's my last hope to make this deal happen.

"It's a good thing we didn't let him use one of his vintage cams." We both laugh. Jared is a connoisseur of analog photography, says we've lost the art with all this technology.

"The upside to digital," Chloe says, smiling.

I laugh again at thoughts of our eclectic friend.

"Yes, we still get the picture with digital."

It's quiet for the moment, and I realize I haven't told Chloe how beautiful she looks in royal blue. She's a tall drink of water with long blonde waves that cascade around her face. A Scandinavian beauty queen. I feel like a dwarf standing next to her. "You look really nice, Chloe. I'm glad we're doing this tonight." She pats my hand and we both look out her passenger window.

As expected, the rush hour traffic is a parking lot, and our five-minute drive is turning into 25 minutes. Our driver finally pulls up to the curb and we're greeted by a wall of screaming fans. Already they've lined the red carpet, nine people deep.

Chloe pays the cabbie with a bundle of scrunched-up bills from the bottom of her clutch and glances at me. "Should we just go in?"

"I'd like to take pics of some of the celebrities for our blog." I'll load them up if we actually land this costume deal.

"Sure, sure," she says, winking at my unspoken

obsession with Julien. She interlocks her arm with mine, and we walk toward the crowd like two lovers.

"There," Chloe points, and I see a bald spot among the mass of people. It's near a camera crew, and they, too, have insider passes to the event. We'll follow them in after the red carpet fanfare and let them clear our path. Our exclusive passes, along with the way we're dressed, should wield us some importance while cutting through the crowd. The rest of the onlookers are dressed in summer tanks, and Bermuda shorts.

Chloe's height acts as a royal pennant marching us into battle. With one hand, she holds her event pass which hangs from a lanyard around her neck. She raises it high near her face, like we're Secret Service. With her other hand, she pulls me through the crowd.

I love her. She's the sister I never had and always wanted. Chloe believes in me, just like my mom does. I'm going to make this deal happen, even if I have to sell my soul to do it.

Our spot is three feet from the camera crew, leaving them wide birth to move around. I'm pushed up against the gray metal barricades, and my ribs are bruising from the weight of the crushing crowd behind us.

Chloe stands slightly behind me and closer to the camera crew. She wants me to be the one to get the photos.

"There!" She nudges my arm.

Julien comes around the corner with his entourage. The artsy cliques and star-struck groupies roar at the sight of him.

The man is beautiful. Judging by the giggles of the women around me, I'm not the only one who thinks so. He's an assault on all my senses, and I sway on my heels.

He typically wears black, thick-rimmed wayfarers, but not today. Today, I have the rare and unobstructed view of his stark green eyes. His lashes are black and so thick you'd swear he wears guy-liner.

Julien stops for photos and gives the audience a curt but affectionate wave, acknowledging their outpouring of love. His eyes are gracious yet narrow, like those of a predator, as he scans the crowd. Am I the only one who sees this? Julien Wolfe is a wolf dressed in couture.

"Wow," I murmur.

"And look, he has no date." Chloe leans down and angles me a little, since she's technically closer to him. "Grab your phone."

My fingers fumble at the bottom of my clutch purse. While my forearm is angling for room against the metal barricade, I manage to snag my phone between my fingertips. I hit the display. Jared hasn't texted back, and I still have no idea if he has backups of our photos. I inwardly sigh and open up the camera screen.

Julien's now standing 10 feet away.

My purse hangs from my shoulder, and the

event lanyard hangs from my neck. I'm a mess of straps and ribbons. Everything I'm holding looks gaudy against my gown but is a necessary evil to enter the movie premiere. I flip my pass behind me, so I don't end up tangled and miss the photo-op of Julien when he passes. The square plastic now sits on my back, the corners scratching at my shoulder blades. From the front, I bet the red canvass ribbon looks like a choker.

He's closer now.

I'm trying to stifle my hammering heart so I can get a good shot of his face. Julien's a trim man with a swimmer's build, though from here, I can see the way his tux stretches across his wide chest, the fabric protesting around his biceps and shoulders. He's devastatingly beautiful. I'm relieved for the barricade's assistance in keeping me upright.

Julien's perfectly mussed hair is the colour of onyx and matches his bowtie. I clench my jaw, wanting to bite the tie off with my teeth. I fan myself, pretending it's the heat of September making me warm. I'm behaving like a smitten 16-year-old trying to kiss the poster of some boy-band crush.

I must be infatuated with the man. Not just for his work, but for everything he's about and everything he seems to hide. There is something hidden deep within Julien, something I want to uncover, yet I'm nothing more than a fan—and hopeful future business associate. There will never be a romantic relationship between us, and I need to get that into my dreamy head now.

My mom says that women building their empires don't get tangled in matters of the heart. Sex yes, love no. And now I understand why. It's alarming the amount of space Julien takes up in my brain, and I've never even met him.

I take a few snaps with the zoom on. Julien has stopped to shake hands and sign a few poetry books. I check my phone again, and still there's nothing from Jared. If I don't get those design reprints, we're positively screwed.

He's closer now, and the crowd behind me heaves in anticipation. It's pushing me harder against the barricade, and the bottom of my ribs feel like they'll break through my skin and hook onto the metal bar.

Soon we can go in, I tell myself, ignoring the squishing of my intestines. Inside we'll have general seating, and I don't care where we're placed, just as long as I have a clear view of my idol.

There's a hard tug on my event pass between my shoulder blades. My body is wrenched backwards and my lanyard grows taut around my neck. I start to choke. "Help," I try to say, but I can't talk...or breathe. My hand latches onto Chloe's forearm. She's too busy looking left at Julien and his crew to notice.

Julien's two steps away now, nearly in front of us, and one of two things is about to happen: one,

I'm going to miss seeing him pass by on account of blacking out, or two, I'm about to choke to death smack in the center of an oblivious crowd. I'm seeing stars now, black dots float across my vision, and I'm teetering on my stilettos.

Chloe's still smiling and hugging her purse to her chest, and my hand on her forearm is weakening.

I attempt to turn my body to see who's trying to steal my pass into the event, but people are standing so close to me that I can hardly move. They can't have my event pass. It's useless to them. My name's on it. With my neck muscles clenched, I manage to take a mini-step back and turn, taking pressure off my trachea. Now my back's to Julien, but at least I'm getting oxygen to my brain, and I'm not going to faint like a fool or die a pathetic death in the middle of the film festival. I'd prefer to be alive than look like an idiot dying in front of the man I want to jump.

Slowly my vision comes back into focus as I take a few deep breaths. I can't see who's trying to kill me over this piece of plastic. I can only see a hand protruding through two clueless bystanders.

"Oh my god!" Chloe yells, finally figuring out what's going on. "Let me help." She pulls on the lanyard, toward my chest, making the crowd heave toward us. It's like we're trying to pull a gargantuan onion deep from the earth, except the dirt is a throng of bodies.

"You can't have it!" I croak, leaning all my

weight backwards. In the next breath, my arms are wind-milling as the metal clip connecting the pass and lanyard bends and breaks.

Then I'm falling backward.

I reach for Chloe's hand and miss it by inches. My back hits the hard steel, and the heavy barricade topples away from me and toward the red carpet. It's going down, and I'm going to land on top of it.

This is going to hurt.

I hear the fabric of my dress tear on the metal spindles. The pain leaves me breathless. Stars explode from behind my eyes, and I want to faint from the agony. I don't think I'm bleeding, but I can't catch my breath as I lie sprawled across the downed barricade. Tears prick my eyes, and I don't want to open them. I'd rather die of embarrassment than acknowledge the amount of pain I'm in.

"Oh my god, Amelia!" Chloe yells.

I feel someone grab my hand, and I'm relieved. Chloe's there to save me from any further embarrassment. She'll hide me, shelter my tears, and help clean me up. Everything's a little strange right now—that must be why Chloe's hand feels wider and hairier than I remember.

chapter four

"ARE YOU ALL RIGHT, MISS?"

I recognize that deep voice from the countless interviews I've PVR'ed. It cuts through the pain, making my head swim. It's like silk being dragged across my bruises. I brush the hair from my face and look up.

Julien Wolfe.

Holy mother of…

The crowd starts clapping, and like a champ, I raise a shaky hand, acknowledging that I'm fine. There's nothing I can do. Everyone's seen me fall, and hiding my embarrassment will only make me look ridiculous. Security bustles behind me to resurrect the barricade I've just toppled. And now I'm standing on the red carpet like an insider, with my best friend, the man of my dreams, and a ripped dress.

"Are you all right?" Chloe's frantic.

"I'm fine." I can't hear my own voice over the crowd. My arms start to tremble involuntarily, and then my legs, and I can't figure out what's the matter with me.

"She's in shock," Julien says.

My body hurts, but I can't tell if the shock is from holding his hand or from falling.

Julien's staring at me with worried eyes the colour of dark forests. A dark forest full of secrets, I remind myself. But I know this man. I know his poetry, nearly word for word. I know this movie we're about to see, how it's about his tumultuous relationship with his father. I know where I am. Everything is fine.

Julien gives me a gentle smile, and I'm blinded by his unexpected kindness. I look down to find I'm still holding his hand. He chuckles.

"I'm sorry." I let go of his hand like it's just burned me, and again I push back the lock of hair that has fallen in my eyes and shove it behind my ear. "Sorry, what did you say?"

His brow wrinkles with concern. "You don't seem all right."

Chloe nudges and hands me my clutch. I slip the strap over my shoulder and notice my lanyard with its missing movie pass. Julien's security team escorts Chloe inside.

I hold up my haggard lanyard. "I don't have my—"

Julien takes me by the arm and interweaves it with his. "You're now my date for the evening. You don't need a piece of plastic. I'm admitting you inside, Amelia."

"That's me," I say, as if he's taking attendance.

He pauses, and a look of amusement stretches across his face. "Come." And though I'm sure he meant nothing by it, I feel like I'm about to. "I want to make sure you're okay. Besides, you'd be doing me a favor by saving me from talking to industry stiffs."

My heart sinks but I still manage a brief smile. He wants me to sit with him—yay! He wants to do it to make sure I'm okay and keep people off his back—pooh. I remind myself that I'm only sitting with the man of my dreams for a couple of hours; it's not a marriage proposal. I need to get my head on straight. I'm a professional businesswoman about to pitch to this man's company in three-days. It's not a date. It's *not*.

"All right," I say, straightening my shoulders and adjusting my dress. I've torn the slit up my thigh, which now rests too high on my hip. "I appreciate your hospitality, Mr. Wolfe."

Julien stops short, and I nearly run into him. He turns to face me and for a few seconds, he looks annoyed. I blink.

"I'm going to call you Amelia, so I expect you to call me Julien, please."

"Okay, then. Julien, it is."

He takes my arm again, and normally I'd protest at the firm grip, but I still feel wobbly. Inside, the press swarms like locusts, and more flashes blind me. Julien points to an area of the red carpet that veers left. It's the corporate sponsor area for the festival, the banner that acts as a backdrop for press photos. He asks me to wait with Chloe while he goes off for some necessary media shots. I take that moment to check my phone again, to see if Jared has texted with the status of the photos. *Nothing.*

I lean in inconspicuously and whisper to Chloe. "I saw you with Julien's team. You didn't tell them who we were, did you? About the pitch Monday?"

Chloe's staring at Julien as he has his photos taken. "Are you crazy? Of course I didn't. But my goodness, Amelia, he picked you up off the motherloving barricade!"

I'm trying to forget visions of me making a complete fool of myself as Chloe yanks to break a stray thread at my hip, where my dress tore. "We get to sit with him," I say.

"I know! His team told me." Chloe is excited, and I am too, but something's nagging at me.

Maybe I should tell Julien we're pitching to him on Monday. On the other hand, I don't want to ruin the moment, and what if Jared doesn't have the photos? I could be wasting an opportunity to spend time with Julien. The only time I might ever get.

He's being interviewed by one of the TV tabloid entertainment networks. They call him "Mr. Wolfe" too, and his scowl is darker than the one he gave me. His female publicist scrambles at the look on Julien's face and gives the press core a one-minute warning.

Chloe whispers in my ear. "What the heck just happened?"

"I don't know," I tell her. But for the love of all things holy, there's something about using "Mr. Wolfe" that sends him around the bend, and I'm not about to ask what that something is.

"Maybe we should just go and get ourselves a drink," I suggest.

Suddenly Julien's publicist is at our side. She's a petite Asian woman and though she doesn't look it, my guess is she's a little older than Chloe and me. Her hair is long and hangs pin-straight down to the middle of her back. She's thin and her dress is strapless and formfitting with Chinese blossoms down the front. She's captivating and looks as if she just stepped out of an art gallery in SoHo.

"I'm Lillian," she says, with a thick London accent. "Love, I'm sorry about what happened earlier."

I shrug as if it's no big deal, like it happens every day. A waiter holding a tray of stemware heads our way. He's nearly past when Lillian picks up two glasses of wine and thrusts them under our noses. Lillian then lunges to grab one of her own, before the man can glide away. "I don't know about you but I think we all need a sip." She clinks her glass against ours before emptying the contents in one long swallow.

I glance at Chloe. Julien's over there taking photos for the media and Lillian's standing here with us. "Don't you need to tend to—"

She waves her hand.

"No, Julien is very much in control of his messaging and personal brand." But then she darts back just as he finishes his photos, picks up her clipboard and starts talking with a reporter.

Chloe gives me a puzzled look, and I open my mouth to respond, but something catches my eye in the periphery.

Julien's finished with pictures and walks toward us. My eyes don't know where to look when he zeroes in on me. It's hard to concentrate. I have to hang on to my train of thought so I don't trip over myself like some idiot damsel again.

Seconds before Julien reaches us, he's intercepted. A bald man and two macabre looking women start talking to him. Dread settles over me. I turn to Chloe, who looks equally sickened. We know these people.

"Derek Wiggleby," I hear our ex-boss say with an outstretched hand to Julien. But my poet-slash-movie-director doesn't seem terribly impressed. His eyes shift to me—he wants me to save him, as per our agreement. But I can't bail him out without blowing my cover. I don't want Julien to know I'm a costume designer, and Derek is a jerk of epic proportions. I can't let him see us.

I turn my back, pretending to scope for the ladies room, hoping Derek doesn't spot us. Chloe and I walk towards the washroom and duck into an alcove, watching the celebrities attending the event.

"I can't believe he's here." Chloe's voice is filled with disgust, and rightfully so. In our fourth year at the Theatrical Institute of Design we had an internship at Wiggleby's, Derek's costume house. It's a small firm, certainly not as small as our little start-up, but it's busy and profitable. We'd still be there if Derek didn't want to sleep with all of his employees, both men and women. Including us.

We were dismissed upon graduation, not landing a full-time position despite our high marks and rave employment reviews. He's now our competition. Wiggleby's isn't as specialized a design house as our Amulet Designs. Derek is considered a generalist and does all kinds of movie production costumes. I'm hoping our corset niche will give us the advantage on Monday. If we make it to the pitch, that is.

"Alrighty then!" Derek's voice cuts through the noise. "We'll see you on Monday, Mr. Wolfe." I cringe at the formal use of Julien's name, but I don't dare look at his reaction.

"We need to land this account," I say to Chloe. "We need to bury him."

"Yeah, but what if Jared doesn't get back to us with the digital proofs?"

Her words give me pause. I haven't thought of what we might do if Jared doesn't come through. I still have the corsets, but we'd need to hire a model to wear them for new photos, and that's a cost we absolutely can't pay right now. Julien's team won't accept sketches — only hard samples and photos.

I feel heat along the left side of my body. Chloe's eyes widen, focusing on a spot behind me. A warm hand is holding my elbow, and I glance over to see Julien looking at the underside of my forearm, a look of disapproval on his face.

"You're bleeding," he says.

I glance at the spot in question, and it's only then I feel the stinging cut from my fall into the barricade. It isn't a large gash, and most of the blood has dried already, but it's terribly unattractive and only reminds me of the embarrassing debacle. "Chloe!" Derek's annoying voice cuts again through the crowd, and my fantabulous friend steers him away so he can't see me.

In the next breath, Julien conveniently pulls me into a corner, tugging a handkerchief from the breast pocket of his tux. I don't know what he's planning, but the bloody gash on my arm has partially dried. I give him a questioning look, but he doesn't notice me. He holds my elbow up, licks the handkerchief and works the dampened fabric along the dried blood, staying clear of the cut itself.

I'm riveted by Julien's intense focus. As if he can feel my stare, he glances up. His eyes fix on mine, then drift to my lips.

"You've the loveliest mouth," he murmurs. "I could write sonnets about that mouth." He gently lowers my elbow but doesn't let go.

"Now, Ms. Amelia, if there is to be anymore

falling this evening, it will be into my arms. Is that understood?"

I swallow hard. I'm incapable of speech. The man is potent and sexual, and I've nearly orgasmed three times tonight from his stare alone. I'm a businesswoman behaving like a complete moron.

A flicker of lights in the main corridor signals it's time for us to take our seats. Extracting my arm from his hold, I thank him for his help, waking both of us from his spell.

"I should sit with Chloe," I tell him, because it doesn't matter how smitten I am — chicks before dicks.

"Chloe can sit with us. We have enough seats," he says. "But make no mistake, it's your company I want this evening."

I don't mistake anything. The deep baritone in Julien's voice, leaves me speechless and smile in agreement. I want his company, too.

Not My Father's Hands describes his father's life from the time Julien was born, his father's fame as a movie director, to Julien's mother's murder and then his father's own suicide. I was in my early teens when newswires lit up with the scandal. Mom knew Julien's mother from industry events, but she never spoke of the woman. There's no hint of his mother's murderer in the film. I suspect they'll never know who did it.

The movie is nearly over, and Julien's hands are gripping the armrests of his chair. His upper lip is dotted with sweat. For his sake, I try to play it cool. Though at one point in the film — the scene where his father launches a beer bottle at the wall behind a young Julien's head — I grabbed hold of his wrist. I'm thankful he squeezed my hand in that moment. It's as if he, too, is seeing this film for the first time.

The final scene is dark, showing his father hang himself. The man's only remedy to his drug and alcohol addictions, spurred on by the murder of his wife.

The credits roll, and the audience sits silent. Then it starts. A lone clap rising into a crescendo of applause. There are whistles, and the crowd stands in ovation and turns to face Julien. He suddenly looks uncomfortable and humbled. This isn't just any film — it's personal. The praise must feel bittersweet. I want to hold his hand through the long ovation, but he isn't mine to soothe, no matter how much I'd like to comfort him.

"They loved it," I whisper in his ear. A small nod of his head tells me he's heard.

He puts his hands in a prayer position, gives a small bow in appreciation and waves. They continue to love him with their cheers, while Julien looks down at me and winks.

Once we file out of the theater, the sky is deep indigo and fading into black with a crescent moon. There are stars, but in the heart of metro we don't see them. Just the light from the buildings and landmarks.

Julien has asked that Chloe and I stick around. The lobby is filled with glitzy dresses and tuxes, many of them making an exodus to the cavalcade of limos out front of the theater.

"Oh my god," Chloe mutters out the side of her mouth. "Did you see the way he looked at you in there?"

I did, but I don't want to make a big deal of it. "I'm sure it was nothing." Julien's a famous celebrity, a businessman, but he's also a human being who is uncomfortable with praise about his work on such a personal and sad project. I did what anyone would do and helped him through it, that's all. I would have lent a hand even if he were a total stranger.

Chloe abruptly pushes me behind the sponsor's banner. "Shh," she whispers. Then blocks me in, leaning against the wall as if she's waiting for someone.

Derek Wiggleby walks by, his staff flanking him. "I have no idea who we're competing against on Monday," he says. "Not that it will matter. We're the only costume house large enough to meet Wolfe's needs."

I want to laugh in his face. What Derek doesn't have is Chloe and me. Chloe was the top seamstress in our class and has an eye for eclectic detail. Together, with my penchant for corsets, we are a force in historical clothing design. That's why

Derek hired us while still in school—well, that, and who my mother is. I grew up with concept sketches resting on the breakfast table. I'd play in the swathes of fabric on the floor of mom's sewing room. He doesn't have the education about the craft and information about the industry imparted to me.

"We need to win this," Chloe says, and I can't agree more.

My phone buzzes at the bottom of my clutch, and I scramble for it, hoping it's a text from Jared. It is.

"OMG! I gave you my only flash drive Amelia and saved copies to my desktop. That storm power surged me and wiped out my hard drive! Sorry, Doll. I lost all my client photos, I'm fucked."

My heart sinks and the tears threaten. We spent all we had on those pictures. Jared gave us a deal because we're his friends. He's struggling like us. I know he can't repeat that deal. And I can't fault him for not backing up his files differently. He's in just as much trouble as we are.

Chloe sees my face as I put my phone away. She doesn't have to ask what happened. My best friend will be forced to go home to live with her dad in Yonkers. I can't afford to stay in Manhattan alone. Mom says that, as an absolute last resort, she will employ me. But that's not what I want. Nor is it what she wants. I want to make my way, make my own name, and I want to do it without anyone knowing I'm her daughter.

Earlier Julien mentioned something about an after party, but I don't want to go. I want to be taken seriously as a contributing member of the film industry, not some groupie who has latched on to the director. But the loss of those pictures means I'm screwed. All I want to do is go home and get drunk. In my pajamas. Then tomorrow, during my excruciating hangover, I'll figure out what the hell I'm going to do with my life.

Chloe nudges me, and I look up to see Julien.

"Can I speak to you for a moment?" he asks. Before I can answer, he steers me into the alcove near the restrooms. His eyes lock with mine, and he looks like he's assessing me. "I keep getting this feeling like I know you from somewhere. Have we met before?"

I've known of Julien for years, but there's no way he's known of me. I lived at boarding schools throughout my teens while mom traveled the world on movie shoots.

"No. I don't believe so." My answer seems suffice because he quickly looks over at Lillian who's fast approaching. She whispers something in his ear and then she's gone.

"I want you to come with me to this party tonight."

I glance at Chloe, who is standing by herself, looking as lost as I feel, and there isn't a thing we can do about it.

Julien follows my gaze. "Chloe can come too."

My mind is a battlefield. Thanks to the storm

and my lost files, tonight's the last time I'm ever going to see Julien. I want to go home, slap a nipple on a bottle of wine I can't afford, and nurse my sorrows. Yet, I want to be close to him, even if only for a few hours.

"Can I run it by her?"

An amused look creeps across Julien's face. "Of course."

On my way to Chloe, I notice my statuesque friend is picking her cuticles, something she only does when she's nervous. "What are we going to do, Amelia?"

My face scrunches up, and I look down at my scuffed stilettos that were pristine when we first arrived. I need to be honest with her. "I haven't the foggiest. We won't be ready to pitch on Monday. We may need to shoot for another project in a couple months, once we get our costs under control and build up some cash to start again."

The words taste rotten as I say them. My dream of working with Julien Wolfe is slipping from my grasp. He wants corsets and historical wear. That is our niche. If we can't get a big job under our belts, we can't expand our line, hire more seamstresses, and bid on new deals. If this movie, which will hit screens in the next 18 months, goes well for Julien, he may do a sequel.

I glance back at Julien who is talking to his staff, and his eyes meet mine. He's serious, he wants us to go, and something about his gaze tells me he isn't going to take no for an answer.

I turn back to Chloe. "Julien wants us to go for a drink. I think we should go. It may be the only insider event we're invited to for a very long time, and it's an opportunity for us to mingle with some industry people."

Chloe lifts her purse. "I don't think I have enough—"

I place my hand on her forearm. "My mom says drinks are always free at these things, Chlo."

She sighs. "Maybe you should just tell him we're supposed to be pitching to him on Monday."

I had thought of that, but gauging Julien's reaction to Derek Wiggleby's slimy pre-sales pitch earlier, I get the sense this isn't the time or place. My mom always says these functions are to introduce yourself, schmooze, and collect business cards. A chance for people to find out whether you're likeable, but never to actually pitch. "Did you see the way Julien looked at Derek when he started talking about the pitch?"

"Point taken."

"And anyway, we have to accept that we won't be ready on Monday. Let's go to meet other people and learn about other upcoming projects." Until now, I haven't voiced the possibility of not pitching next week, and by the look on Chloe's face, she's trying hard not to show her disappointment. "While I'm entertaining Julien, why don't you mingle, see if you can meet some other directors?" She pauses for a moment. "Well, we are dressed up."

I know she's in and before I can say anything Julien's at my elbow again, checking my bruise. "Everything set?" he asks, shaking his head at my cut, then lifting his gaze to mine. It's such a tender gesture, one I'd never expect. I tell myself he only wants company for the evening, a distraction from such an emotional movie premiere. But there's something in his eyes that feels like he needs me.

chapter five

OUTSIDE, THE STREET LIGHT BOUNCES OFF THE IVORY cast iron buildings of the historical, posh neighborhood. I'd kill to live in the area, but $10,000 a month in rent is not in my realm of possibility.

Julien rides in a limo ahead of us. Three of the actors from *Not My Father's Hands* are with him so when they exit the car, they'll make their entrance to the party together. We pull up near the front of the Metropolitan Hotel. It's also the location for Monday's pitch. I wonder if this is where Julien's staying while he's in town.

Inside, the after-party is broken up into three different rooms along the mezzanine. One room is akin to a smoky urban bar with cabaret seating. Another is fashioned like a dark nightclub with neon-colored laser lights. The last room is a candlelit lounge with low leather couches and dirty martinis.

At first, everyone's corralled into the urban bar. It's dark and the round tables are filled with industry professionals, while partygoers cluster around the periphery. On the stage sits a single microphone and a lonely bar stool. A guitar rests upright in its stand, the rose-colored stage lights illuminating the dust motes. Lillian greets the audience and sounds the praises of the film and its soundtrack. The crowd applauds.

A woman takes the stage, a recording artist adorned in a gypsy skirt and fitted tank top. She's lanky, blonde, and earthy. She strums the title track for the movie, and it's dark and soulful. I'm transfixed by her gentle voice. I feel Julien's eyes on me, but I don't want to look. Lusting over Julien is a dead-end. Not only in business but emotionally, too. How did I get here? When did things become so complicated? Julien Wolfe is the type of man to lead a woman toward self-destruction. I pushed hard for this project and it's falling apart. For the first time I can admit that I don't think we're ready. Should have stuck to small theater for a while. How I didn't see it until now, I'll never know.

Since it's so dark and we're standing near the bar, it will make for an easy escape to the next room, once the set is finished. I feel the heat of Julien's body next to mine. His forearm grazes the small of my back, and his hand is held fast to the wooden counter on the other side of me. His breath is warm on my skin just behind my ear. It's intoxicating. And as much as I try to focus on the stage, I'm losing purchase. Nothing's right in my world, and I'm about to be homeless. The thought leaves me cold and I take a step closer to Julien. If he wants to be close tonight, I'll take all the warmth I can get.

When the applause dies down, Julien slides his fingers along my nape, and I can't help but turn in time to feel his searing lips, pressed against my skin. I want to tuck myself into him. Thinking better of it, I reach for my wine sitting atop the bar, just as the slow lick of Julien's tongue leaves a small, wet trail along my shoulder. My eyes drift shut.

Dear god, Julien Wolfe's lips are on my ever-loving shoulder.

The audience resumes clapping and Julien's tongue is gone as fast as it arrived. My skin is left cold and wet. My eyes open, and my body shudders, missing the warmth of his mouth. There's a pull on my waist, and we're whisked into the nightclub. He clasps his fingers with mine, and I should tell him it's too much, too close. That we were meant to work together, not hold hands, but my mind is a mess. At war between two dreams. One dream of working for Julien, and the other of sleeping with him. What is the matter with me? Why can't I see my way between fantasy and reality?

Julien stops to talk to a few people, pulling me along with him. Chloe is up ahead with his bodyguard. They're laughing and chumming, and she punches him in the arm, making him laugh. Their dynamic is laced with friendship, and mine is laced with infatuation.

"Here," Julien says, handing me the fourth glass of wine I should be declining. I'm already balancing like a manic ballerina. If he asks me to dance, he'll need to hold me up.

Chloe isn't fairing much better. She's bouncing to the beats and hugging a tumbler of what looks to be vodka. I'm happy that she's taking advantage of the open bar and meeting whomever she can.

Just as my best friend peels onto the dance floor with the entourage, Julien takes my hand and escorts me in the opposite direction, through the maze of pedestal tables and barstools. I'm pulled into a dark, private corner. Julien angles me so my back's against the wall and places a gentle kiss on my lips. Before I can even think, my palm is at the side of his jaw, and I'm deepening our kiss.

What the heck am I doing?

Before I can say anything a wide-eyed Julien takes my face into his hands. "Jeezus, Amelia, who are you?"

I'm the girl you were supposed to work with. As thoughts of being a failure spiral through me, my resolve unravels. My heel slides up the wall and I open my legs. Julien fills the small space between and with an urgency I can't explain, I pull his lips down to mine and devour his mouth. His forearms rest against the wall at either side of my temples and I'm caged between his hot body and the wall.

If I can't make one dream a reality, I can make another happen.

I've wanted this man since my freshman year, and at this moment he's staring into my eyes like I'm the only one who exists in this fucked-up world.

After seeing his film tonight, I know he too, has been living in the eye of a storm. He seems just as lost and vulnerable as me.

I whimper as he pulls me close, his breath dancing along the shell of my ear, making me feel more drunk than I already am. "I feel like you were sent to save me tonight. Isn't that weird?" His voice sounds gravelly and dark, and I nearly soak through my lacey thong under the onslaught of his words.

My eyes dart to the dance floor. It's bright there, but not where he and I are standing.

"I want to fuck you, Amelia."

I meet his gaze and swallow his words. I want him too. I want him hard, I want him fast, and I want him right here. Julien takes my lips in a fury and leans his weight against me. His sex is like iron and pressed against my pubic bone, sending fissures of lust up inside my belly. I grab hold of his waist, and we're gasping loud over the pulsing beats, savoring the rapture rushing through our bodies.

He runs his thumb along my bottom lip, looking like a man trying to get control of himself. "You seem like a respectable woman, and I'd be no man to fuck you in the middle of a nightclub. Still, I want to see you come. You're so damn pretty." He brushes the hair from my eyes.

I shift my gaze to the dance floor until he angles my chin again, my eyes again fixed on his. He takes my mouth, and his tongue teases mine. His other hand starts burrowing, his fingers inching through the tear of my dress. His fingers are warm, seeking until they find the scrap of lace covering my sex. He cups me through the mesh.

"You've soaked your panties." His hand holds me firm, and I feel my wetness leaking on to his fingers. With eyes closed and foreheads touching, we both moan.

The music is slow and sultry with acid beats. My body's no longer mine to command — my mind has slipped past all rational thought. With eyes closed, I throw my head back, lost in some kind of carnal bliss.

"I'm not going to take you here, Amelia, but I want to be inside you, want to see you come, want to taste you."

Both disappointment and mischief wash over me. Seconds ago, I'd nearly orgasmed just from the idea of having him inside me and I'll settle for whatever he's offering. This morning my dreams drove away on that bus, and come two weeks I'll be out on the streets.

Losing myself emotionally is the release I need tonight.

"Please." I beg him.

Julien lifts my triangle of lace and burrows his large hand between my legs, forcing me to widen my stance. In my ear he whispers sweet exaltations as the music rises. He dips one finger inside me, then two, then three. I'm riding his hand, and he's shoving his fingers inside me slow, then fast.

Julien's sex is hard against my hip, and I want to come. His lips are on my neck, hot like a brand, and I can think of nothing but chasing the wave of lust between us.

"Fuck, I never imagined you like this." I say.

Then he takes my lobe playfully in his teeth, and he's growling and working me with adamant thrusts of his hand. Desperation surges through me, and I take his face between my palms and devour his mouth. Forget slow sips, I'm consuming him, and he responds with furious fingers and his thumb at my clit. My hips undulate, wanting to chase my orgasm. There's a slight tug on my hair and a feral look in Julien's eyes. This is the Wolfe. This is the one I suspected lurked beneath his skin.

Julien's taking back control. And I want nothing more than to turn over the reins over to him. Everything I touch falls apart.

"Please," I beg again, without a hint of embarrassment. I'm no longer a potential business partner, but a wanton groupie with his fingers crammed up inside me. I don't care. This will be the last time I ever see him.

"Siren," he whispers against my lips and plucks my breast from my dress. My hands plunge into his hair as his head dips to take my nipple in his mouth. He pulls at me with long, greedy sucks. "You're close, aren't you?"

I mouth my yes.

Only a few more minutes pass, and I feel myself making my orgasmic ascent. His fingers are moving in and out of me. I break our kiss and close my eyes, my face tilted towards the ceiling. I can see the pulse of laser lights beneath my eyelids, and I bite my lip to ride the sensations.

"So fucking soft," he says, and with renewed vigor he presses the heel of his palm right where I need it. My body starts to writhe, and Julien's right shoulder is pinning me against the wall. He swirls his hand in a firm, circular motion with the perfect amount of pressure, and I'm close, rising.

When I'm at the cusp, he shoves the fourth finger in and bangs his unyielding hand into me. As my scream is drowned out by the deafening sound of the nightclub, Julien continues his assault, wringing out every last jolt from my body.

My forehead falls to his shoulder, and I'm panting, trying to catch my breath.

"Fuck. You're a stunning woman."

Breathless, I fumble to reach for the fly of his tux. And when he stills my hands, I look at him like he can't be serious. "Rain check," he says.

He must see my disappointment. He runs the

back of his fingers along my cheek. "Don't worry, love. I intend to collect."

He kisses me in the centre of my forehead and my heart sinks.

Because there won't be a next time.

chapter six

"WAKE UP!" CHLOE YELLS, SLAPPING THE LIGHT ON in my bedroom. I want to kill her. My brain feels like someone is slamming doors inside, and my body feels like it's been put through a rock crusher.

I fling the covers over my head. "Leave me to my misery." I feel the bed dip and the weight of her sitting, pinching my blankets against my hip. "What do you want?" I whine, not letting the harsh lighting at my corneas.

"Jared's been calling you. Your phone's dead again."

I stretch my arm out from beneath the covers and slap my nightstand in search of it. Chloe hands the phone to me.

"It's not dead." I tell her. "It's off."

She mutters something about my irresponsible habits, and I roll over and face the wall, ineffectively dismissing my friend. A corner of blanket is yanked off my head, bathing me in the disgusting sunshine cutting through my window.

"Get dressed. He'll be here in about twenty minutes."

Excitement rolls through me. My body jackknifes and the covers pool at my waist. "Why? Did he retrieve our proofs?"

"No," she says and leaves the room.

I roll back over. "Turn off the light on your way out." It was silly to get excited. There are no more moves left in this play. My fate was sealed last night when I let Julien Wolfe put his hand in my lace and make me writhe in public like a wanton woman.

Chloe comes back, places a cup of coffee under my nose, and slowly I like her again. "So, you want to tell me what happened last night? The minute we got in the cab you passed out. I could barely get you out and up the front porch. I don't want to think about how many pounds I lost getting you up to the third floor."

I look down and realize I must've fallen asleep in my strapless bra and panties. My evening gown is draped over the arm of the mannequin in the corner of my room. I stare into the contents of my mug. "Sorry you had to take care of me."

"Not as sorry as I was getting you undressed. You're so thin but you weigh a ton."

I take a sip of the coffee. It tastes like tar on my alcohol-weathered tongue. I'm feeling dehydrated and could go for something salty for breakfast.

"Like I said, sorry." I give her a sheepish grin, and she bats her hand as if it's no big deal.

"So spill it. While I was getting you into the car last night, Julien was grilling me for your phone number so he could text you today. Something about sending his homemade remedy for a hangover."

My heart melts a little at his thoughtfulness. But I can't see Julien again, not after last night. "You didn't give it to him, did you?"

She looks at me like I'm nuts. "*No*. Silly. I gave him mine, and he's already texted three times. That man's intense."

"I can't see him again, Chlo. Did some nasty things with him in the nightclub last night."

She looks horrified. "You didn't."

I close my eyes and sink against the headboard. "We're pooched. Game over. I've been crushing on Julien Wolfe since I was 12. If I couldn't achieve one dream, I was hell bent on achieving another."

"Look, we've agreed since our days working at Wiggleby's that we don't sleep with bosses or coworkers."

She's right, but... "I didn't sleep with him, and you and I both know we won't be working with him anyway. We can't pitch on Monday."

"Oh geez, Amelia. Jared's on his way over with a solution that might work."

I don't get excited. I can't think of what Jared's possible solution could be. I push my hair behind my ears, take my mug in two hands. "I'm listening."

"Jared's coming with his equipment. Right now.

He's bringing white sheets to drape over my bedroom. We're taking new shots of all the corset designs."

Poor Chloe, still scrabbling for a solution.

"We can't pay him. I don't even know how we're going to make rent in two weeks, let alone pay for last month's."

Chloe stands and pulls my draped gown from the mannequin, threading a hanger through it. She hangs it in my closet. "He knows all that. He's doing this pro-bono. He feels awful about not having his files backed up."

He should feel bad. What kind of photographer doesn't back up his files? The same kind of person who lacked the common sense to back up her design files online, that's who. Seems common sense is not so common at all. I'm a hypocrite. A hypocrite who feels sorry for herself.

"His offer's generous, Chlo, but even if he did get us new photos, we don't have a model."

Chloe is too tall to wear the corsets, and she won't fit the bust anyway. They weren't designed for a woman of her figure. We'd have to make eighteen new corsets to fit her size two body, and we don't have that kind of time.

Chloe lifts an expectant brow.

"Oh, no. No way. I've already done enough damage to my reputation. You can't possibly think I'm going to do it."

"You owe me," Chloe says, playing the ultimate guilt card.

I can't have my face on these shots, and then present to Julien's team with any sense of dignity. I do have some integrity, even if it seems like I don't.

Chloe rolls her eyes. "We knew you'd say that. So Jared is only going to shoot you from the neck down."

My crafty friend goes on to tell me not to wash my hair. Our neighbor downstairs, who's a junior stylist at one of the top salons in the Bowery, is on her way over to put my tresses up in hot rollers. Then she's going to stay the day and do some body makeup thanks to my spill on the red carpet last night. And of the bruises she can't cover from last night's fall, Jared will photoshop.

I can't believe I'm actually considering this. Not to mention that I have to look at Julien, at his hands, knowing where they've been. Suddenly I feel the need for another drink.

I sit in our small kitchen with can-sized rollers atop my head. The light shines in from the front bay window—Chloe's bedroom—where Jared is setting up his silver umbrellas and draping white linens over the bed and secondhand furniture.

"Perfect, perfect," he mutters and pushes back his black faux-hawk back with electric blue fingernails.

Our neighbour has me sitting in my nude body sock. It's strapless and will sit beneath each corset.

She's spraying my skin with one hand and with the other she's dabbing me with a sponge to feather the lines.

Chloe's lining up all the boned corsets on top of a train of towels sitting outside the bedroom. They lay along the length of the hallway, stiff, like medieval body armor ready for battle.

This is fitting. I feel like I'm heading into a battle zone of questionable morality.

Julien's upcoming film has a time travel plot. The movie begins during the Renaissance in 15th century England and finishes in Denmark in the year 3010. The corsets range from sexy peasant to black leather of a femme fatale. Then there's the other costumes they've asked us to illustrate.

"Tell me again why I need my hair done if we aren't taking pictures of my face?"

"We need to humanize your photos for effect, so we'll take pictures of your full body from the back. Your hair will add contrast to the photos in a big way."

Then we begin.

The shoot starts with my red hair hanging low. First, pictures of the corsets, starting with most contemporary and ending with historical. My hair hangs down in loose waves to the middle of my back. We finish with my hair up in a loose, disheveled bun, like I've just come from battle. I'm fitted in tight, black leather pants and a matching black leather corset that stops above my breasts.

The shots Jared takes from the back are provocative and teasing. He jumps around, crooning praises.

"Amelia, you should have modeled these from the start!"

No. I shouldn't have. I'm the owner and one of the designers. Modeling's not my bag, but I'm desperate. It's then that I take my first look at my breasts and cringe at the way they swell, lusciously overflowing my bust line. I know this effect. I designed the corsets to look this way for my models and the actresses, to be sexy and alluring.

But on me...I'm shriveling with self-consciousness. I'm not a model or trained to think like one. Those women are professionals.

The day progresses into lace-up corsets in various fabrics, from corduroy and canvas to frayed satin. My hair sits high now. Sloppy waves fall down to my nape and tickle the column of my neck.

The final corset is off-white, laced up the back, and dirtied around the grommets—leftover teabags age fabric nicely. The piece was designed as something to be worn by a lady-in-waiting, someone bustling around and working in some high-society home, just as the script's synopsis suggests.

The outside grows dark limiting the natural light spilling in from our windows, so we decide to clean up. Jared takes out his laptop and hooks it up to my projector. He shines the images against the white walls of our flat. The four of us fall silent and stare at the photos.

Jared has a sudden intake of breath. "Perfection."

"Oh, Amelia." Chloe is awestruck.

The simplicity and elegance of the photos can't be disputed. Not showing my face adds to the allure of the designs and brings out the quality of our work. The model we originally hired was blonde. My orange-red mane makes the colors of the corsets pop. I'm ashamed to admit it but the shots are better than the originals.

Chloe breaks the mesmerizing moment. "Hot damn! We're so getting this deal." She claps her hands together and hugs them to her chest.

"I so need to be your ongoing photographer for all your projects," Jared says. "You are a force, my friend, and after today, I wonder if there is anything you can't do."

I give them a bashful look. It's not like me to feel embarrassed about good work, but today I can't help it. We've pulled off something truly extraordinary. We stare at the final image, the one of me in the black leather corset.

I wish we were pitching tomorrow. We're ready now. I'm no good at having time to sit and brood. I have the jitters about the whole thing and just want to land the deal and be done with it. But tomorrow's Sunday, and Chloe and I have shifts at the lech-filled pub. Then on Monday, we'll meet with Julien and his team in a conference room at the Metropolitan.

We help Jared load up his gear. He and Chloe are laughing and joking, but I'm too lost in the swirling "what if's" to join in. Like, what if Julien wasn't too drunk to remember my face? What if Derek Wiggleby sees me at the pitch and tells Julien who my mother is? Thoughts of mom slide into my consciousness. Specifically, the rumors that her success included "sexually hobnobbing" with industry professionals.

I won't be her.

Good god, tell me I'm not her.

chapter seven

THE SUNDAY TRAFFIC IS LIGHT AS I STEP ONTO THE near empty bus. Crusty puts his hand on his chest with mock concern. "Shame you lost your laptop. You should have said something the other day," he says, finishing with a smirk.

Chloe squeezes my arm, when she sees my hand scrunched into a fist. "Come on now, we can't have you in jail, you need to present tomorrow." She ushers me to a seat.

I take in the space. It's a nice change. There's no hint of body odor wafting through this broken-down hotbox.

My phone rings and the sound breaks through the hum of the bus accelerating.

It's my mother.

"Amelia, I tried calling you all day yesterday to see how the film festival went. Did you wear the green like I told you to? Who was there, and did anyone ask about me?"

This is Claudia Worthington. No *Hi, how are you?* Typical self-absorbed woman with the world at her fingertips.

"Yes, Mom, I wore the green. Though no one knew my name, so no one made any connection to you."

She clucks her tongue. She always does this. I can picture her folding her arms and pouting. "You mean to say you didn't schmooze with Julien Wolfe?"

I don't want to get into it. The more questions I answer about Julien, the more I'll back myself in a corner. When it comes to my mom, omission of detail is the best option. "He was surrounded by his entourage." "Really." Her tone hints she's unconvinced. I don't like the way she says it.

"Really," I repeat, but not before swallowing hard.

"That's funny. There's a picture of you two in *The Post*. A few pictures, actually."

I'm. Going. To. Die.

I want to pull my phone from my ear and check the virtual newspaper, but I can't exactly put her on speakerphone in the middle of the bus. "What pictures?"

"Oh, just one of Julien picking you up off the pavement. Another of Julien wiping your bloodied elbow with a tissue, and one of Julien and you standing at a bar."

I can feel my heart clawing its way out of my

chest. "What are we doing at the one in the bar?"

My mother's laugh is more of a cackle. She's on to me, and I'm about to dig myself into a hole." It's simply a picture of your two heads, looking up at some woman playing guitar. But I will say, Amelia, you two are standing awfully close, considering you didn't talk to him all night."

"We talked, Mom, that's all. I fell, and Julien and his crew were likely looking for a PR opportunity. You know, girl falls, famous director stops to pick her up and make sure she's okay. It's good viral marketing for his movie."

I hope my lie sticks. I can't have her sniffing around my business at this stage in my career. I'm just relieved there's no picture of Julien with his lips on my skin. The nightclub was dark, but clearly people were watching us. I just hope they took a pee break while we were —

"And that's it?" Mom says, interrupting my thoughts. She almost sounds disappointed. "Nothing else happened?"

Thoughts of coming clean flood over me, and then I remember how relentless my mother can be with insider information and her endeavors to help. "Nothing else."

"I can see why he'd be worried on the red carpet in front of all those people, Amelia, but he didn't need to spend the rest of the evening with you."

Chloe is looking at me, wide-eyed and concerned. She knows my mother well enough; the few times mom's been in town, she's taken Chloe and me to dinner. If my mother wasn't a master seamstress, she could have been a prosecutor.

"Mom, he was nice to me. He felt bad that I fell at his movie premiere. Was likely afraid of a lawsuit. That picture you're looking at, where we're standing close at the bar, we had no choice. The room was packed with guests."

"Article says no one knew your name. Says you're some kind of mystery girl. Your guest pass had your name on it, Amelia. How was it no one knew who you were?"

I go on to tell her how my pass got stolen.

"Well, I think you'd make a nice couple."

I cringe at her casual opinion of my love life. If she only knew where I'd let Julien put his hands. "Mom," I warn.

"Don't *Mom* me," she says. "This is how it's done in Hollywood. And before you chastise me, remember I'm your mother and have years of experience when it comes to these things. Don't give me that bit that things are different in New York. The film industry is global." Which makes sense, since she spends six months of every year outside of North America on different film projects. "Couples in the industry get together, share in media opportunities to leverage their presence. They schmooze over dinners and cocktails, and land deals. It's the way it's done."

Divorce rates are also high in Hollywood, but I don't dare start in on how my dad left us before I was born.

"Clearly you were at some parties," Mom says. "Tell me about those."

And there she goes again, like an ape on a banana. If she senses hidden info, she'll peel every last layer until you're totally exposed. "I went to one at the Metropolitan," I tell her.

She pulls the phone away from her mouth to yell at someone in production about the lighting on her heroine's costume and, again, my existence is forgotten for the moment. She's one of the most frustrating women I've ever met.

Yet there are two things I can't refute: she wants the best for me, and she's committed to excellence. She's creative and lively, and I could never imagine her totally absent from my life. "Well, did you at least run into any of your competition?"

I need to watch what I say. If I tell her about seeing my former boss, her questions will lead to my pitch on Monday, which I haven't told her about. She's a viper. If Claudia even smells my hand in a possible deal, she'll do some homework, make some calls, and I'll end up with the job—not on my own merit, but because of her running a campaign behind the scenes.

I've lied to her enough and decide to let this one ride. "Derek Wiggleby was there."

Silence. She knows why I left his design firm. Chloe and I always say, "We don't give head to get ahead."

Someone interrupts on her end to ask a question, then she returns. "I wonder, out of all the films at this festival, why Derek would show up at Julien's premiere."

Shit. She knows about Julien's project, his request for proposals from people in our industry. I already know what's next.

"You know, Julien has the perfect project coming up requesting seamstresses skilled in the area of historic corsetry. It's a time travel film. I wish you were prepared to bid on this film, instead of that idiot, no-talent Wiggleby."

I wonder how many lies I've told her in this conversation and decide to throw down another. "We're too tied up in a small theater project. We—" Chloe nudges me. The bus is nearing our stop. "Mom, I've got to go. I'm almost at work."

"You're too skilled for indie theater, Amelia, and for that ass-pinching sausage party you call a job!"

It's lunch hour.

Plates clatter and bar orders are filled. Eyes sear over my curves, making my stomach roll. I'm not a prude, but I'd prefer to be the object of one man's affections—the one who's been in my heart since my days of braces and bad hair. I feel a hand cup my ass while I carry a plate. My hand swoops down and slaps it without dropping so much as a fork, and then I walk to the back. Bankers laugh at the table I've just come from, and like always, I ignore them. The plates thud on the stainless steel corner in the back. Working in this place makes me creatively numb. My palms rest on the cool surface, and I crack my neck. The men at that table are still laughing, cracking jokes about how I don't miss a beat. I need out.

I so badly want to land this deal tomorrow. Yet why does it feel like if I do, I'm still using my body for monetary gain? Every day I agree to dress in this slinky costume in exchange for generous tips. I glance down at my halter-top. The thing barely covers my nipples.

This motion picture deal is shaping up much the same. I've inadvertently used my body, rather than my talent, to get close to Julien. Yet, I only did it because I thought there was no hope left for a deal.

Julien had his hands all over me, and tomorrow he'll see who I really am. A woman desperately trying to land her first commission. A woman trying to get a start on her career without the help of her body or her mother's connections. Either way, Julien won't be interested in me after tomorrow. I know it. He'll lose all respect for me, thinking I've tried to sleep my way into his world.

"Table five needs a menu," my boss says.

I stop on my way out of the kitchen and slide some menus under my arm. I know table five, don't even need to look up to see where I'm going. My hands search my micro apron for a pen and order book to start them on drinks.

"Well. Hello, Amelia."

The hair on my arms raises. I should have sent another waitress out. His name sits bitter on my tongue, like I've just come from choking down a shit sandwich in the back. "Derek."

His eyes travel over my breasts and bare stomach like he's admiring a new car. He tilts his head to the side and lets out a whistle while appraising the barely concealed curve of my ass.

His eyes feel like centipedes on my body, and I grit my teeth. "Can I start you with a drink?" *Idiot?*

Derek leans back in his chair, then *tsk*'s. His eyes hold fast to my exposed navel as if he's in pain. "I've always been interested in any fluids you have for me to drink. I think I'd like a body shot from that rockin' body."

I throw up a little in my mouth and painfully swallow the stomach acid back down. "So, a glass of water?" *For your lap?*

He laughs. "Oh, Amelia, this is too fun. I just came by to offer you and Chloe your old jobs back. Was so impressed with the way you worked Mr. Wolfe the other night." He winks at me with one of those beady eyes I'd like to remove with a spoon. "Or, should I say, the way he worked you?"

I swallow hard. No one saw us in that corner and Derek was nowhere near that after party. No one would have invited him. But the fact Derek knows I was there leaves me unsettled. We live in a world of smartphones, and there is no privacy. If he's got photos, he could professionally bury me.

"Relax, Amelia. I'm the only one who saw what

happened with you and the sly Wolfe in the corner. You're a vision when you're in the throes."

Oh god.

After a beat, I try to up my bravado—like I don't care—but I'm mortified. I slip my pencil above my ear with a huff and shove my order pad in my apron. I leave to fetch him some water. It's the distance I need to come up with a decent response that won't get me fired. I decide to ignore his comment. Derek may have seen us, but it was too dark inside the Metropolitan. There is no way he could prove it. I return to him with the pitcher.

"Derek, thank you for the job offer, but Chloe and I have jobs."

He looks around the pub, a look of knowing amusement on his face—as if he expected me to reject him. "I see that. And what a fine way to make a living. Say, if you like the uniform so much, I'll let you wear it under your work clothes and you can parade for me after hours."

It happens so fast.

Derek's hands fly straight in the air as I empty the pitcher of iced water on his lap. He's in shock, and I can't bring myself to feel bad about it. I thought waitresses only did this stuff in movies. Not so. Satisfaction warms me until I notice the restaurant has grown quiet.

And then I hear my boss. "Amelia!"

chapter eight

THE LOOK IN CHLOE'S EYES WHEN SHE LEARNS I'M being sent home and taken off shift rotation for two weeks is a level of disappointment I never want to see again.

I keep failing her.

I make the walk of shame until I reach the bus. The ride seems louder and especially lonely without my best friend. A friend I could really use right now, but who needs to keep working because of my foolishness.

Crusty barks at passengers hopping on the bus, and I wonder if anyone would notice if I toss him into oncoming traffic and let a Mercedes have its way with him.

I need to look at this suspension as an opportunity to prep for tomorrow's pitch to Julien's team. Jared has offered to lend me his laptop. I perish the thought at fumbling with an unfamiliar piece of equipment in the midst of an already nerve-wracking presentation.

With everything that's been happening, I haven't had a moment to read Julien's poetry page this weekend. I keep telling myself this, but truthfully, I'm afraid to look. Afraid to continue falling for a man that I shouldn't fall for. This obsession needs to stop, and cold turkey seems the only viable option. Yet in this moment, I want to read his words because they inspire me.

My fingers travel swiftly across the screen of my phone, and without conscious thought I've pulled up his poetry page.

There's a new poem.

THE GIRL WITH THE HURRICANE EYES

I swear she fell from the sky.
Sent from heaven to hold in my empty hands.
An angel with hurricane eyes
Brilliant irises the color of fresh cut grass
Hair like a lick of flames,
Hanging low, the soft tips kissing her shoulder blades.
A dusting of freckles that I swore held all the
constellations of the gods.
Her beauty pulled at me, and I was honored to clean her
wounds,
Never once expecting her to do the same.
The way she held my heart while it was ripped from
my chest from watching the silver screen.
I don't know her, and yet,

K.T. FREDERICK

I wanted to hold her, and
The more I held her,
The more I wanted to bury my face in the hollow of her
neck,
To whisper all the ways I needed to surrender myself in
someone
And how in that moment
I wanted desperately for that someone to be her.

My phone flies toward the center of my chest, and my eyes dart around the bus, as if my fellow passengers know what I've just read. I cross my legs at the wetness that's slipped from my sex and pooled in my panties. I'm aroused in the middle of the bus, and I quickly put on my sweater to hide my titillation, which I know is on display. Judging by the vacant stares no one has noticed that I've nearly orgasmed on a cracked leather seat.

My heart bangs against my ribcage, and I look down to read the poem again. He couldn't be talking about...he couldn't be. I have hair like a lick of flames, and my wounds...he did say I was saving him that night, but... I try to push away the thought, but something in my conscience niggles. Julien could have been writing about me.

He posted it last night while we were

reviewing the photos with Jared in preparation for tomorrow's presentation. Again I tamp down the idea. Julien can't possibly be writing about me. The man likely must have an exponential number of women at his mercy. This man has me muddled up, and I need a clear head to navigate us out of this mess.

Finally home, I enter the kitchen and find Jared's left his laptop on our kitchen table with a note of good luck. He left me specific instructions for tomorrow's presentation, along with two extra flash drives of our photos.

My bag falls to the floor with a thud, and I sit alone in one of the two bistro chairs. I run my fingertips along the seam of the closed laptop. I feel deflated because I've become my mother. I've inadvertently but unequivocally become her, and I'm ashamed. My first possible client, and I've pandered my body because I felt sorry for myself. I don't even recognize me anymore.

The front door slams shut, and by the cadence of shuffling feet I can tell it's Chloe. She's home three hours early. If she isn't at work, whose making money so we can stay in this apartment another month?

She storms into the kitchen but doesn't look at me. The cupboard door squeaks open and she reaches for a bottle of pills. "Man, I've got a headache."

"What are you doing here?" I don't even try to hide the bewilderment in my voice.

"What? We've got to land this account tomorrow!"

I stand next to her, and my eyes are riveted to the way she's guzzling a massive glass of milk. "Why are you home so early?"

"Got myself suspended, too."

I feel my eyes bug out of my head. "What happened?" "Dumped Derek's plate of food on his lap when he touched my ass." She looks sheepish. "Can't say I blame you for what you did to him. I'm sorry for being so hard on you earlier."

I let out a laugh, then hug my best friend. If this is rock bottom, we're in it together.

And if we're about to meet our doom, well, we're going to do that together, too.

chapter nine

THE BOARDROOM AT THE METROPOLITAN IS SET
somewhere in a labyrinth of hallways. I'm wearing
my black pantsuit with a charcoal-steampunk
corset beneath. My hair is tied back tight in a low
bun; my oversized glasses and muted makeup
complete the look. I'm a far cry from the lusty minx
of Friday night.

Chloe is dressed much the same. Our collective
look is respectable. It says we stand by our product,
yet are conservative enough to conduct a business
meeting.

I glance at my phone. Nine on the nose. No one
sits on the fancy leather benches in the hall outside
the meeting room, which means we're likely the
first team presenting. My stomach is flipping end
over end, and I'm desperately trying to hang on to
my breakfast, which Chloe implored me to eat.

The double doors open, and I recognize

Christine Winters, Julien's assistant director. She was there on Friday night. Part of Julien's entourage, but too wrapped up in the evening's events to notice me.

"Good morning," she says all business, no hint of recognition. "If you'd like to set up, Julien will be with us shortly."

In a way, I'm relieved I don't have to face Julien alone, that I have time to get my bearings before seeing him. Chloe glances at me with that worried look. I give her a nod, letting her know it will be fine. I've put us in this mess, and I will do whatever it takes to get us out.

The boardroom sits 12, but there are only four people milling about the far end of the oval table. They, too, are waiting on Julien.

Chloe rushes to set up, and the room dims when Christine pulls the drapes behind her closed. Darkness. Bonus. With renewed vigor, I take my place at the front, slightly off to the side and out of the direct path of the light projection. I'm but a shadow with a voice; the highlighted screen the focus. This just might work.

Amulet Designs is scrawled in large print across a presentation slide, with our names A.P. Jacobs & C.J. Matthews in smaller letters beneath.

Light floods into the room when the door is thrown open and I remain quiet and hidden in the shadows. It's Julien. He gives a small wave and takes his seat across the room, next to Christine. We can barely make out their shadowed faces, which tells me they can't see ours. *Perfect.*

"All right, we can begin now," Christine says. "Thank you for coming in today."

"Good morning," I say, standing straighter. "I'm Amelia Jacobs. I'm here with my partner, Ms. Matthews, who you'll hear from shortly. We are Amulet Designs."

There's a cough at the back of the room. "Excuse me, what did you say your name is?"

Crap. I purposely didn't mention Chloe's first name, as Julien would've surely recognize us before I finished the pitch—how many other Amelia's and Chloe's could possibly be running around New York City? I pray he doesn't figure it out now.

"Amelia."

He's reclined in his swiveling chair, tapping what looks to be a script with his pen. His staff doesn't dare prompt him to move on. From the light of the projector, I can see the lower half of his face. He purses his lips. "All right, thank you, Amelia and Ms. Matthews. Please carry on."

Julien runs his index finger along the soul patch of sin sitting just below his lip. The sight of his fingers and the thought of where they'd been on Friday night makes my throat dry and I cough.

A quick sip of water and I begin discussing the durability of our costumes and their ability to hold up under aggressive scenes. I talk about period pieces and various fabrics. How they won't fade under production lighting, how every piece shown today can be reproduced with modifications, custom-fitted to the actresses.

I'm only three photos in when Julien interrupts.

"Slower, please." His voice is suddenly deeper and husky. Julien can't possibly know it's me. Thanks to Jared, the photos show none of my freckles or my bruises.

"Of course," I say. Then quickly address some questions from Christine about the English designs.

Near the end, I flip to a photo of one of our more futuristic costumes. If Julien puts it together at any point, it will be now, with this shot. My hair is down, and my red mane is in stark contrast to the black, tightly fitted leather. My eyes dart to Julien. The calm demeanor is gone. His body is stiff and he leans forward with his hands clasped tight, like he's just putting things together. The words in his poem about my hair being a lick of flames slam into my frontal lobe. *Dear god, he knows.*

Christine and Julien speak at the same time, interrupting one another. Then Julien sits back, and says, "Please," and opens his palm, encouraging his assistant director to speak first. I'm relieved for the moment.

"Amulet Designs is a small design house," Christine says. "Which is one of the main reasons we wanted to see photos of your work, and not preliminary sketches. How are you going to meet the demands of our aggressive production schedule with such a small team? And are you able to make alterations and adjustments on site?"

Blood pounds in my ears. Questions like these will make or break us. I need to forget what Julien may know and give this thing all I've got. I'm the spokesperson for a reason.

Showtime.

"Christine, I've read through the synopsis as well as the scene outlines, character sketches, and set design notes. I have access to additional staff, should I need more to meet your production demands." I don't tell her that most of the "staff" would be fellow students from our graduating class at the Theatrical Institute of Design.

"Your bio says you've predominantly done independent play productions, and that isn't a lot of experience. Can you speak to that?"

"You're right that all of our work has taken place in indie theater. It also means I'm always tasked with working within a small budget. What this will mean to you is that I can keep costs down without sacrificing quality, and pass on these savings to you."

Julien brows raise and he smiles. I've answered appropriately. Christine leans into Julien and says something, then he whispers back. "You're right, Ms. Jacobs," she says. "Cost savings is important to us, but without experience with an existing costume house, we aren't certain about your work."

I don't want to tell them about my work placement at Derek Wiggleby's. I know he'll be presenting next. I don't want to be associated with the man or answer any questions about why I left his firm because Derek is slippery enough to spin a story in his own direction. I won't have a chance to defend myself.

Chloe jumps in. "Umm, could I just say something?"

Christine seems annoyed by the interruption, but Chloe plows on. "I know I'm Amelia's business partner, but I'm also her friend, and I wanted you to know... Amelia was class valedictorian for our graduating year. Not only is she an amazing seamstress, but she completed a double major in school, which included a history degree at NYU. She's never missed a deadline thrown at her."

"I'm sure she's very good Chloe. The problem is the photos would normally be enough to convince us. Your work is beautiful. But it's clear we are your first major deal, so we need to touch the fabrics and see the pieces up close."

She glances at Julien, and he gives one of those Wolfe-ish smiles he's known for. "Our film is a bit of a bodice ripper," she says. "Dammmn," Chloe says under her breath, making everyone break out in laughter.

"The first two scenes take place in England during the Renaissance, and each will have a bodice ripping moment," Christine says. "And two more will happen in futuristic scenes. Which means the corsets need to tear away somewhat easily and show flesh beneath."

"That's quite simple for us to incorporate into

the designs. We'll hand-stitch some seams and use faulty grommets, and I can weaken the faux whale-boning inside," Chloe says. "We'll let you know by the end of today if we're interested. If we are, be prepared to show us samples of some costume corsets that prove what you say they can do."

This isn't the way it's traditionally done. None of it. The interview process, the panel interview, and the need to bring in more samples on short demand. It's not a high concept film, I remind myself, and not like Julien's film we saw Friday night. I'm a gamble for them, and we'll jump through their every hoop to prove ourselves.

Chloe smiles at me. It's her first genuine smile in months. I know I've done right by my friend.

Without warning, Christine stands and pushes open the drapes at the back of the room, and I'm bathed in daylight. Julien's still reclined in his swiveling chair. Pen tapping on the desk in front of him. He's unfazed by my appearance, like he knew it was me all along. When he stands and starts toward me with confident strides, I quickly bend to clean up the laptop and equipment.

"Let Chloe finish the cleanup," he says.

I meet my friend's eyes and her face is apologetic.

We step outside the boardroom, and Julien stands close, like he did Friday night. He's wearing the slightest hint of cologne, and the heat from his body is starting to make me dizzy. I take a step back, giving us a comfortable distance. His eyes dip to the corset beneath my suit jacket and linger on my breasts. He closes his eyes, and sighs before looking up at the ceiling, like he hates himself for eye-groping me.

"Why didn't you tell me Friday night you were bidding on my film?"

This is the moment I've been dreading, and Julien is the only one I feel the need to be truthful with.

"I was given passes to the film festival. It was a fluke that the film showing was yours."

He doesn't look convinced.

"Julien, I had no plans on talking to you that night."

This isn't coming out the way I'd hoped. My skin heats up, and I don't need to look down to know the skin on my chest and neck have turned beet-red.

"What I mean is, if I hadn't fallen, we wouldn't have met until today."

I dare a glance. His eyes are fixed on my collarbones.

"You're blushing," he says, then curses under his breath like he remembers we're here for a meeting. He puts his hands on his hips, making his jacket wing open and stares at some spot on the floor. I shouldn't smile, but Julien Wolfe is showing cracks in his armor. It's nice to know I'm not the only one flustered.

Christine comes bounding out the double doors with Chloe in tow. Chloe takes in the looks on our faces, but Christine's oblivious. "Oh good, was afraid you went too far," she says, smiling back at my partner. "Chloe tells me you're wearing one of the corsets from your collection. Was wondering if I can take a look?"

I stifle the urge to fire dagger eyes at my best friend. "It's just one of my personal pieces from my private collection, but it will certainly give you an idea of the work we can do."

"Can I take a quick peek?"

I can't look at Julien. Already I feel the heat from his gaze as I slowly undo the single button at my waist and peel open my suit jacket.

"Just stunning," Christine says before I can stretch my arms out. "You could start your own fashion line with these. May I?" She motions that she'd like to feel the fabric.

I hold my arms out at my sides.

A vein in the center of Julien's forehead pulsates, and his jaw tightens. Christine runs fingers along the piping at the top, her nails skimming my breasts accidentally. Julien's face looks pained, his eyes following his assistant director's hand.

It feels like Julien's hand on me, touching me, and I'm suddenly aware of my nipples rubbing against the inside of my corset. Christine drops her flattened palm to my waist as she walks behind me with Chloe. The two women talk about the craftsmanship of the corset while Julien and I are locked in a stare. His chest heaves and he runs a single finger along his lip. Like he's remembering Friday night, my taste on his lips.

"Well, good morning!"

Julien and I both startle from our heated moment, and I'm overcome with a familiar dread.

"Sorry Amelia, I didn't see you there. Lovely design as always," Derek Wiggleby says, staring at my breasts. And I don't think I can hate him any more than I do in that moment.

chapter ten

THAT DAY, I RECEIVE THE CALL FROM CHRISTINE AT noon.

"We'd like to see some of your corset samples, so if you could please weaken them, we'd like to run through some scenes and try tearing them from one of your models. Of course, we'll pay for the loss in materials."

I'm smiling like a Cheshire cat, and snap my fingers to gain Chloe's attention. We're a step closer to bagging this deal. I tell Christine how happy and thankful we are for the opportunity.

"One question."

There's something in her voice that brings me back to grade school, a hint of disappointment, and the hair on my arms starts to rise.

"Why didn't you tell us you worked for Derek Wiggleby at one time?"

I get that hollow feeling in the pit of my

stomach, like I've been caught in a lie. I need to say something, and my MO of omitting details hasn't been working for me lately. "Honestly, Christine, I'm not sure what Derek told you, but my stint with him was—"

"Positive," she finishes.

I'm flummoxed. Derek knows I hate him. Why would he give me a positive review? He's up to something. "It's just that my work term at Wiggleby's was short. I didn't think I should add it to my resume. Chloe and I worked there together."

"A year is significant in this industry. The fact that you both worked there helps your case. Don't be afraid to shine. I can tell you're a smart woman. Your time at Wiggleby's is why I asked you for more samples."

She decided? Not Julien? As much as that intrigues me, I'm more concerned with what Derek has up his sleeve. I give Chloe the thumbs up, trying not to laugh at the sight of her doing the running man in the kitchen.

"I'd like you to bring in three samples. If you can weaken them as you said you could and they pass our testing two days from now, we'll give you the deal."

This leaves me short of 48 hours to make this happen.

I look at Chloe who is clawing at my arm. "We'll be there Wednesday for some class-A bodice ripping."

She laughs and for that moment, I swear the

clouds open up. I can tell Christine is rooting for us, and it feels good.

I hang up and share the details. We jump, holding each other's hands like a couple of 16-year-olds who've just been asked to the prom.

"Well, I can help," Chloe says, referring to her suspension at The Hen. "Not like I've anything better to do now!"

Here we are living off fumes, throwing everything at this deal to make it happen, and she's still encouraging me and smiling. I tell her about the glowing review Derek gave about our previous work for him.

"No!" Chloe's horrified, like she's just noticed a spider crawling in my hair. "I don't like it."

"I know. He has something planned." We continue on about how Derek saw Julien and me against the wall at the party. "Now he knows we're bidding on Julien's deal."

"Short of your mother, you're the best corset maker and historical costume designer on this green earth. Christine and her team will see this. Don't worry about Derek."

I'm suddenly less concerned about presenting to Christine's team. I know our work will meet her expectations. It's Derek's change in demeanor that still has me reeling. At one time Derek loved my work, raved about it more than once. Then he sent Chloe and me packing with some scathing comments — payback.

"There's something not right, Chlo."

"Don't worry about it," she says. "When we land this deal, Derek will feel like an idiot for not renewing our contracts when he had the chance."

My cell rings again. I don't recognize the number but decide to pick it up, in case it's someone from the production team. "Hello."

"Amelia, Amelia." The merriment in Derek's voice makes me want to launch my phone against the wall. "Lovely seeing you at the pitch this morning."

I don't want to say a thing. "What can I help you with, Derek?"

"Well, my little prodigy, seems you've had quite an impact not only on Julien, but on Christine. Thought that man was going to burn a hole through your tits outside the meeting room today. So naturally I told them of your work stint with me."

My eyes drift shut. He is disgusting. I pray he hasn't said a thing about my mother. "What did you tell them, Derek?"

"Oh, nothing in particular. Just that you are a fantastic designer specializing in corsets, but that they're your only real specialty. And that I'd be suited to handle the rest of the costumes on set."

The words fly out of my mouth before I even have a chance to stop them. "You know that isn't true! We can handle all the pieces for the movie. I've put it in my written proposal, so they know too. Even wore some of the gowns and blouses in my modeled photos. Christine's been to my webpage, she knows we can do all the costumes, and I talked at length about them." I'm blathering, but I can't seem to stop.

"Oh, I know you can do it, but this is business. I've a proven track record. I'm also counting on you hiding that you're Claudia Worthington's daughter. Self-righteous thing that you are, you wouldn't want to hitch a ride on mommy's coattails."

Chloe's standing right next to me, mouthing the word *fucker*.

"What do you want?"

He chuckles, and I want to reach through the phone and choke him. "Thought you'd never ask. What I want is for you to land the deal with Julien's film."

My eyes dart to Chloe. This doesn't add up. I put my hand over the phone receiver and tell her that he wants us to land the deal.

"No way," she hisses, "Slimy McSlimeington is up to something."

I uncover the phone. "And?"

"Why would you assume the worst of me?"

"Because you *are* the worst, and you're clearly working an angle. Spill it."

Instead of answering me, he calls to someone in his office. "Muffin," he whines. He should be the star of a sexual harassment case in a legal textbook. A few moments of silence and he finally perks up. "You will land this deal with Julien, and I know this because the man had his hand down your panties. I'm sure Ms. Christine doesn't know about that, and I'd hate to accidentally attach my photos in an email to her and the tabloids. The ones of you and Julien getting it on in the corner of a bar."

I'm frozen.

"What do you really want?" I bite out through clenched teeth.

"I want you to land this deal with Julien's team. Then I want to buy your firm for one dollar, so I can have you and Chloe back—and your deal with Julien."

This is why businesswomen don't fuck their clients or bosses! *For this exact reason.*

"So, why don't you tell me where you're at with this deal," he goes on. "Tell me what still needs to happen for us to close it."

I walk away from Chloe and sink to the bed. My voice has lost its fire. "I have to bring in more samples this Wednesday."

"Darn," he says. "I have a business meeting Wednesday. But do check in with me right after presenting. Tell me how we did. All right, dear?"

The man has called me his *little prodigy* and *dear* in the span of three minutes. I'm his fucking pawn.

"Guessing by your silence, I've given you a little to think about. So why don't you just get those alterations ready, and we'll talk again on Wednesday afternoon."

I open my mouth to respond, but nothing comes out. Tears prick my eyes, and Chloe rips the phone from my ear. "Hello?" she yells. "Hello!"

But it's too late. Derek's already hung up.

chapter eleven

CHLOE ENDS THE CALL AND I CRACK. I EXPLAIN everything to her in a blubbering mess of snot, high-pitched mumbles, and tears. She pulls me to her chest and lets me cry for a few minutes.

I finally sit up, and she looks down at her now see-through white shirt. "It's okay. Wet t-shirt contest is this afternoon."

I'm failing us both, and she's making me laugh. "What are we going to do?"

"We're going to go in and make it happen. We're going to find a way to land the deal, and then we're going to find a way to keep it out of Derek's grimy hands. Worry about step one before worrying about step two."

"But what about—?"

"No buts." She shakes her head. "We need this deal. We need you to land it at all costs. It's our survival. There's a piss-pot full of money at the end of this rainbow, and we deserve it. Let's worry about Derek once we've landed the deal."

Part of me wonders if I should tell Julien about Derek's threat, but I want to save him from this debacle. He's got a movie to direct, and he's finally gotten away from years of negative press.

Chloe can see where my mind is headed. "We'll visit whether or not to tell Julien after you've landed the deal."

I wipe my eyes with the backs of my hands.

"Let's get to work," she says.

We pull the laptop over and start scrolling through the images. Then it hits me. "We don't have a model to wear these corsets on Wednesday. Do we know anyone willing to have their clothes ripped off for free?"

Chloe looks at me and matter-of-factly says, "Yes. You'll wear the corsets."

I'm already shaking my head as the words come tumbling out of her mouth.

"You're the only size six here and you're the only one prepared to work pro-bono."

I can't believe I'm giving serious thought to her suggestion. The level of professionalism I'm displaying has officially hit rock bottom.

"What have we to lose?" she asks.

I stare at the Broadway poster hanging on the wall. My last hope is to show Julien's team my designs can be ripped from the body of a not-yet-casted actress.

"I can't," I tell her, shaking my head. I've a limit

to my loss of dignity. This isn't how I plan on getting ahead. My gaze drops to my palms. I don't even recognize who I am anymore.

"Fine," Chloe says, throwing her bag on her shoulder. "Blow everything we've worked for, not to mention our savings and dreams. You're not your mother. She slept with whomever she needed to, in order to make things happen. You're not her."

I suddenly wonder if my mother fell into the same trap as me. If she made blundering mistakes that made it look as if she were sleeping her way to the top. Was she constantly falling and getting back up again? When I was small, she was a penniless, single mom. Back then was about survival and she did what she had to. Just like we are, now.

Chloe puts her hands on her hips and leans forward. I've only ever seen her do it twice in all the years I've known her. I'm about to get it.

"You think you're the only one who's ever done something idiotic in pursuit of a dream? Think you're the only one who's made a mistake in the midst of heartbreak? The difference between you and everyone else is that *they* turn it around in the second act."

It's 2 a.m. My fingers are tender. Weakening the seams on these corsets takes an exorbitant amount of meticulous hand sewing. It's time-consuming, but thankfully not all seams need to be adjusted — just enough to weaken the durability of the garment. Proving we can turn this around within 48 hours shows we can handle any short-order work on set when the time comes.

Chloe turned in an hour ago, but I can't sleep. I head to my room with an oversized mug of chamomile and Jared's laptop, which I'm thankful he has not asked for yet. Tomorrow we'll return to the Metropolitan with the corsets and let some actor rip them from my body to prove our worth. This is more than a test of my skills; it's a test of my flexibility to act under pressure. And I'm ready.

Once my night-shirt's on, I slip into bed. The laptop's on my nightstand, and I eye it warily. Haven't fed my Julien addiction in two days, and I'm dying for a bump. I flip open the laptop and hit the start button. At first I get a message – *404 page not found* – and I panic. He's taken his website down.

I refresh the screen. Nothing.

There has to be a different browser already loaded on this laptop, so I find one and give it a shot. This time, the website comes to life. I click on the poetry tab. A heated knot forms in my stomach at the sight of a new entry:

SPARK

I perished
while the burning embers of yesterday cooled.
I searched for you, for a hint of flame.

That only dimmed with the passing hours, and
then died within the fire pit of my stomach.
No word, no call.
Just a first name.
Yet at dawn, among artificial shadows,
a spark of hope.
Patience clawed at me,
Desire strangled me,
Until light thrust upon the situation.
Then she was there,
and sirens blared.
My fire roared.
My flame had come back to life.

Poem by: Julien Wolfe
Post: 985

The bus is especially ominous Wednesday morning.

Chloe is abandoning me. She needs to get to Grand Central and rush home as fast as possible. Her dad's been taken to the hospital with chest pains. I fire her a nervous look, feeling selfish. The look is partially for her and her dad, and partially because today decides our fate.

"Amelia." Chloe reaches for the back of my hand and squeezes. "I would be there with you if I could. I need to be with dad."

I give a little wave of my hand. Of course she does. Like mom and me, Chloe and her dad have only each other. Both of us raised by single parents, this is what unites Chloe and me.

She sees me glance at my phone. I want to reread Julien's most recent poem to help me forget about the flutters in my stomach.

"Don't even think about it. You've got to put that man out of your head for the next few hours, at least. You know there's a very good chance you can't ever be with him romantically, right?"

"I know," I tell her. Yet, I can't help but wonder if his last post is about the presentation we gave to him and Christine on Monday. "Do you think he could have been writing about—"

"Let's not go there, it's the last thing we should be talking about."

"You're right," I say. "I'm putting him out of my mind. Forever. Lusting over Julien Wolfe won't pay our bills."

We finally arrive at Union Station, where the mass of commuters bustle towards subway, bus, and train. Chloe hugs me, her voice strained. "You'll land this. I know you will, and when it's done, we'll figure out what to do with Derek."

I straighten my shoulders. I will land this. I *will*. "I won't let you down, Chlo. I'll make this right."

One final squeeze, then she slowly backs away and waves until the crowd swallows her whole. I turn towards the subway platform. My goal is to stay as sweat-free as possible. Christine and Julien don't need me looking like Sweaty Eddie modeling corsets this morning.

The subway ride is uneventful. My mind in a perpetual loop of dread and confusion over what I'm about to do. I'm trying to win a high-end costume contract with such amateur tactics. The wheels on my large suitcase—which holds three bodice-ripping corsets and skirts—clicks along the sidewalk. I manage to arrive with only a little dew on my brow.

Until now, I had never noticed the majesty of the Metropolitan. It's a little intimidating. The building sits on one of the busiest corners in the Tribeca neighborhood. Everything is brightly colored with dark trim. Classic lines mixed with old charm. The guests are as sophisticated and urban as its architecture. It's the trendy, go-to spot for A-list celebrities and royalty when they come to Manhattan.

I square my shoulders—no one's going to make this happen but me—and push through the double doors with renewed vigor. I'm Amelia, costume designer to the motion picture industry. I'm the unknown daughter of the Oscar-winning Claudia Worthington. I'm a past designer at Wiggleby's. We will land this deal.

I arrive at what I think is the rented boardroom in the basement of the hotel. The placard outside reads J.W. Productions, confirming my destination. The doors are open, but the lights are off. No one is here to meet me. No Christine and no actors sipping coffee. It seems terribly informal, but I want to be here early to set up and have time to change into my first corset.

I pull the luggage in one hand and set it upright just inside the door. This has to be the wrong room. I step outside again and snag a hotel worker pushing a cart down the hallway. "Excuse me. Is this where the meeting is for J.W. Productions?"

"Yes ma'am," the worker replies. "Set this room up myself last night. Mr. Wolfe came down from his suite to double-check that the tables were arranged the way he wanted them."

I enter the room again, and this time I look for the light switch on the wall. The back drapes are pulled open, and daylight floods the room. Julien turns around with a tight expression, his hands on his hips.

"Julien." My voice is far too breathless for a business meeting. I clear my throat.

"Good morning, Spark."

I give him a gentle laugh, fold my arms and give him a questioning look, like I don't know what he's talking about. "Spark?"

He doesn't elaborate, so I let it pass. We need to keep this all business, and getting into his pet names for me isn't wise. My eyes traces his shoulder down to thin binder tucked between his elbow and his body. The script. The script I have yet to see. Julien's stare is unwavering, like he's memorizing my image.

I quickly divert my gaze to the facilities at the

front of the room, since that's where I'll need to change.

Then it occurs to me. "Where's Christine and the rest of your team?"

"She had to fly back to L.A. We have some set design conflicts she needs to take care of."

"And your actor?"

He gives me a puzzled look. "We haven't casted the male or female lead yet. It was going to be Christine or myself handling the testing of your work this morning."

It's just Julien and me.

Julien is going to be the one to tear away the fabrics from my body. There was never going to be an actor. And I'm the model. There was supposed to be a room full of people, and now it's just us.

He glances at the door, then back at me. "Where's Chloe?"

"Her father's sick." I thumb towards the door behind me as if she's just on the other side. "He's been taken to the hospital."

"Is your model on her way?"

Okay, this one's an outright lie, no omission here. "She cancelled on us at the last minute, something about a broken ankle. So, uh—I'm the model today."

Julien's nod is slow. His eyes flicker with a new understanding—we're alone in this. Just Julien, me, and three flimsy corsets. Corsets he's about to tear to pieces.

"If you'd prefer to reschedule, Christine will be back in two weeks."

Inside, I want to reschedule. Wait until my friend is here. But our rent is due in a week, and we need the deposit for this job. I can't wait.

This is it.

I make light of the situation. "It's all right. I have a body stocking I wear beneath. We can do this today."

"I'm going to lock the door then. I don't want anyone thinking I'm attacking you."

"Ha, right." Holy shit. But if we're following the scene notes, we need to do it this way. The general public doesn't know my fabrics are auditioning for a movie role. Closing that door is wise. Totally a sound business decision.

Okee dokee, here we go.

chapter twelve

I COME OUT FROM THE WASHROOM WEARING MY first corset with the skin-tone body stocking concealed beneath. The corset is an English Renaissance piece that laces in the front and has a hidden zipper buried in a side seam.

I glance down at my breasts. They're pushed up, and my ample cleavage nearly spills over the top, as designed. My nipples are just this side of safe. My waist is cinched, making me the quintessential hourglass. Until now, these corsets have been nothing to me but works of art. Fabrics and lace over which I've slaved. But now I feel as beautiful as an actress is meant to feel wearing them. I'm proud of our work.

I don't know where I'm supposed to stand. I look up at Julien, and his gaze is dangerous. His fingers are gripping the corner of the table, like he's losing any semblance of control. My skin turns pink under his gaze but instead of demure, I feel powerful and sexy.

"You're a beautiful artist," he says, his eyes fastened steadily to my waist.

Out of everything I display, he compliments me on my artistry. As a professional artist, I relish the opportunity to partner with one so equally passionate about his craft. I say thanks, and Julien picks up his screen notes.

"If you could stand over here and face the table," he says. "In this scene, Romano, our villain, comes up behind the heroine and attempts to ravish her from behind. He reaches around the heroine from the back to front, then pulls the corset down and away from her body in the front." Giving the camera a money shot, I imagine.

Images of Julien ravishing me with his fingers flit into my head, and my gaze accidentally drifts to where they hold his notes. I feel my cheeks flush and I quickly look away. This whole thing is absurd, unconventional.

In reality, I'd have a model. In reality, actors would be testing out the costumes on set. But our reality is it's an independent low-budget film, and they're giving my upstart company a chance.

I stand in the narrow space between the table and Julien. The heat coming from his body is intoxicating. He maneuvers behind me, hands slipping along my waist. They feel hot through the fabric. His breath is warm against my nape. His scent makes my body thrum to life and my sex begins to weep.

"Are you all right, Amelia?"

I realize I haven't been breathing, and my eyes are closed. I know if I talk, all my words will come out as a squeak.

"Let's get this over with, then," he says, and with both hands he pulls me tight to his hard body.

My back hits Julien's chest, and a gust of air escapes from my lungs. His one forearm fastens me to him like a hot bar above my breasts.

"Now you need to try to pull my arm down and away from your body with both hands, like you're trying to escape."

I reach up with both hands, taking hold of Julien's forearm, his crisp shirt sleeves are rolled to his elbows.

"Now struggle," he says, low in my ear. "Try to break my grip."

I don't wait. I struggle, and he lets me. Everything is boiling up inside me as I twist in his hold and pull at his arm. I hate the situation I've put Chloe and myself in. This isn't acting. I'm struggling for this deal, fighting to make something of myself, and angry at how I've gone about it. But I'm not just fighting for me. I'm fighting my unyielding attraction to Julien.

"Amelia," he says. He's breathless, and his erection is pressed into the small of my back. He likes when I fight him. He's getting aroused. I do it more. A whimper accidentally escapes my lips.

He hisses in my ear as if I'm torturing him. Just then his other arm slides up my bodice and he runs his hand over my breast. His thumb glides across my nipple, hunting for any hint of arousal through the thick fabric.

I come undone.

I struggle harder and moan, pushing my backside hard against his length. I need him to rip this corset off and get me away from his body. Or I'm going to do something I'll regret. "Please," I beg with a voice I don't recognize. "Do it. Please."

It happens fast, the impact instant.

Cold air hits my chest as I pitch forward toward the boardroom table. Julien is there behind me with one arm around my midriff to catch my fall. I'm holding us upright with my palms flat against the table. We stay like that for a moment. He's panting, his forehead against my upper back.

After a silent minute, he straightens and pulls me toward him.

"Are you all right?" he says, his lips pressed against my hair. It's an intimate hold he's got me in, and I don't want him to let go, but he needs to.

I tell him I'm okay, and too soon he releases me. We don't look at one another. The reminder of why we're here hits me and I turn so he can inspect the carcass that used to be a corset. It hangs from me, my body stocking barely sparing my dignity.

"That one passed the test," Julien says, and returns to his notes, writing...something.

I walk briskly to the washroom again, to change

into the second corset. The piece is still of the Renaissance period but Italian in style. It's a maroon lace-up bustier, which is short in the bodice and stops under my breasts. I'm wearing a long white billowing blouse beneath, which scoops at the neck. My breasts sit in the hammock of the fabric. It's a sleek yet seductive look. I've weakened both the blouse and the bustier corset for this next experiment. I come back out to the testing area.

Julien's eyes dart between my breasts and waist. I hold the sides of my long skirt out, giving me the look of a fan below the waist. He runs a frustrated palm over his mouth, then pulls his eyes away to check his screen notes. "This next scene has you up against the wall," he grunts, then clears his throat. "But your back is to the wall, you're to be facing me this time."

"Okay." I point to the barest wall. "Here?" I don't want to assume what's appropriate for the scene.

"Sure." He walks toward the wall ahead of me, avoiding my gaze.

I follow.

My heart feels like it's pounding out from my blouse. Julien angles my body the way he wants, with my back to the wall, arms over my head. He holds one forearm beside my ear, and reads his notes with the other. Ebony hair dances across my nose, and it smells of citrus and spice. I close my eyes and take him in, only to open my eyes and find him staring at me with a smirk. *Busted.*

"So what do you need me to do?" I say, hoping to reset the moment back on business.

"Stay leaning against the wall, but lower one arm and place it behind your back. You're supposed to be secretly struggling with a small knife hidden in your skirts. The camera will get a shot of that."

I do as he asks.

"Now, the other hand needs to be above your head. I'm holding that hand tight against the wall."

And then I do the math. Julien's free hand is going to tear the clothing from my body, and the thought of him doing it again is far more erotic than it should be.

"Are you ready?" he asks, and I tell him yes, trying hard not to look at him.

He takes my chin with his fingers, angling my face toward him. "No, you need to look at me in this scene."

I can't fathom why. I'm just a stand-in, not the actress. But I don't argue, I want this deal.

I look at Julien, and instantly I'm drowning. The man has forests in his eyes, mysterious and green, and I become lost every time I peer into them. I feel my lips part, and his eyes dip to them, as he licks his own.

His grip on the arm above my head tightens. "Fight me," he says, and I think his words should have been *Fight this thing between us*. My body twists and I try to lift my arm from the wall. Julien pushes his body against my hip, rendering me immobile. His erection is like a hot pipe, bruising and rigid, and good god, I want it inside me.

"Fight me, Amelia," he snarls in my face, and his eyes are about an inch from mine. He's barely breaking a sweat. He grinds his sex into my hip, and my fight weakens. Julien palms my breast with one hand; he's taking liberties I should be offended by and he squeezes me through my blouse. Then his fingers are inside the billowy fabric, between my breasts, searching for the top edge of the bustier.

Julien lets out a primal yell, and then it happens.

A massive rip, and the garments are hanging from me. Julien still has me pinned and his gaze unlocks from mine, making its way down to my chest. I look down. My right nipple is staring back at him. Neither of us makes a move to cover it. It's a battle of wills. Julien remains transfixed, then slowly raises my body stocking and tucks me back inside.

I look away, embarrassed. He, too, turns away, and busies himself with his notes. I'm an idiot. This is a business meeting, and I want him to rip off my clothes for real and ravish me right here. "I'll try on the third one," I whisper, pointing toward the restroom and holding my disheveled mess together at the seams.

His eyes are fixed on his notes. He won't look at me. "Sure. We can wrap this up shortly and you can get on your way."

His words feel like a slap across the face. I walk

to the restroom like a woman rejected by her lover.

I slip on the buttery skirt, loosely fitted to my ankles, and matching black corset. It's a smooth and breathable faux lambskin leather. I'm every bit the femme fatale in this number—as if my diet consists of eating men and bullets for breakfast. I love this feeling of power. I leave my hair down and loose around my shoulders, like a mess of flames.

I step out into the boardroom, and Julien drops his scene notes. "Jeezus, Amelia."

This number has officially become one of my favorites.

Julien's stance is domineering, his eyes ablaze. "I know you make your own clothing, but would you wear something like that in public?"

I shrug, making light of his fatherly disapproval. "I might wear something similar at a nightclub. I think I have it in maroon."

There's more cursing under Julien's breath. "Get over here, Spark."

It's a struggle to keep the grin off my face. There's something very heady about unnerving The Great Julien Wolfe.

He angles me so I'm facing him with the boardroom table directly behind me. He reads from his notes. "This next scene takes place in the year 3015. The heroine is a chancellor in the King's court. In this scene, she's lying on top of the dining room table." Julien stops and looks at me, stressing the importance of the scene. "He's, well, expecting her to perform duties which lie outside of her job description."

This time, I can't control a chuckle.

He looks annoyed at my giggles. "Just get on the table and lie face up, Spark."

I do as he asks. At first I let my legs dangle off the edge, but that strains my back. Instead I let the heels of my long spiked boots catch the lip of the table so my knees fall together.

He looks at me and takes a breath. "You need you to spread your legs, Spark."

With a determined chin, I hold his gaze and let my knees fall open.

"Oh, Amelia." He groans and picks up his notes again. I know he's noticed my lace panties, the way my bare flesh peeks out and taunts. He clears his throat. "You need to struggle like in the rest of the scenes."

Before I can tell him all right, Julien's on top of me, bent at the waist, his upper body heavy on mine. His face has transformed and I can't tell if he's in character. Something tells me he's genuinely angry with me in the moment. The synopsis says men turn their eyes away in disgust from the character I'm portraying. They believe she has the devil in her, and judging by this outfit and Julien's expression, I wouldn't doubt it.

My skirt is tented and preventing him from getting too close to me. Julien stands upright, grips my hips, and pulls my bottom to the edge of the table. He pushes my skirt to my waist, leaving me with a corset, black-laced thong, and a pair of tall boots. Before I can even think about protesting, he's back on top of me, covering my modesty. I tell myself it's just part of the script. This is the last scene, the last corset, and then we can finally land this deal.

But there it is again.

Julien's cock is hard and pressing against my sex. Lust infuses my body and I let out an accidental groan. He grinds himself harder against me again, and this time a whimper escapes. Good god, I'm in so much trouble when it comes to this man.

Julien's face is now buried in the hollow of my neck, and his lips are a whisper from my skin. "Fuck, you smell good," he says. "We need to get this over with. Give me your hands."

I bend my arms and slowly raise my hands to my shoulders. Julien pushes them up above my head, and that's when I feel it. I'm entirely at this man's mercy. My breasts are barely contained, and I'm stretched out like a feast. With one hand, he pins two of mine. Suddenly the air is electric. Through his black dress pants, Julien bangs his cock hard against my clit, again and again. My soaked lace is going to make a mess of his trousers if he keeps this up.

"Please." I'm begging again, hoping it cues him to push the scene forward.

Julien growls at my pleading and reaches down with his free hand. He yanks hard on the leather.

This time he's torn my body stocking along with the corset, and I'm bared to him. Cool air makes my nipples pebble, and without rational thought my back arches off the table.

"Fuck it," Julien says, letting go of my hands and his hot mouth latches on to my nipple.

My hands spear his thick hair, pulling him closer to me. He's ravenous and brutal, and it's as if a coil of white-hot tension has finally snapped. Soon he's taken my other nipple, biting and sucking like I'm his last meal.

Then I remember why we're here and I freeze in his hold.

I need this deal, and Julien Wolfe has his mouth on my nipples. What am I doing? "Julien, we can't. I need this deal."

"God, Amelia," he groans against my breast. "The fucking deal is yours."

I'm trying to contain the goofy grin on my face. "You can't give me this deal because we're hot for each other. You'll be my boss."

He releases my nipple, leaving me wet and swollen. His forehead rests between my breasts while he catches his breath. "You're reporting to Christine, she's the one who has awarded you this job. You have this deal because you're a talented artist, a damn good businesswoman, and you did what you said you could do—turn it around in 48 hours."

"Really?"

"Really."

Without thinking, I lift my head to meet his lips and shove my tongue deep in his mouth.

Julien groans at the invasion and digs his elbows into the table to slide further up my body. Kissing me back until I can barely breathe, he says, "For god's sake, Amelia, let me put my cock in you."

I groan out "yes" and Julien pulls the sodden, lacy scrap of fabric between my legs over to one side and drives his glorious fingers up inside me. He starts finger fucking me right there in the boardroom, and my back arcs off the table again, while he sucks and bites on my nipples, ramping me higher and higher.

"Oh god, Julien," I moan.

"Fuck, you're beautiful like this."

I'm not one for cussing, but when he says it in the throes, I feel like I could lose my ever-fucking mind.

"Want to see that body shaking and convulsing, like the other night, Amelia. Haven't got that image out of my mind, and you're going to give it to me again."

I feel like I'm going to come from his brashness alone. My muscles start clenching when his thumb hits my clit and starts rolling it hard in slow circular motions. It only takes a moment, and my breath grows labored. My stomach muscles clench, and my body reclines at a 45-degree angle. My insides ricochet.

Julien grabs me at the back of my neck and takes

my mouth furiously to quiet my cries. It goes on and on, and when it stops he kisses me on the forehead. Then he lowers me back down to the table.

My body is hot against the cold surface, and I'm practically naked, with just scraps hanging off me. Julien's licking his fingers again, and I swear if it were possible, I become more wet.

His arm reaches behind and grabs his wallet. Opening it, he grabs a single foil square. How experienced is Julien that he needs to carry around a condom? I push the thought aside.

He takes the corner of the square and wedges it between his front teeth. His belt buckle is undone in seconds, and the button, fly, and fitted boxers are undone in a tornado of movements. His cock bobs and slaps against his stomach.

There is no way that's going to fit. I'm no prude, but I've only slept with three guys.

"It's okay, Amelia. You're still good and wet, and I'll go slow," he mumbles, the condom wrapper still clenched in his teeth.

Oh right, like that makes me feel better as I'm staring at the drooling python between his legs. In seconds, he's rolling the latex on to his length. The site of him has me pulling my thong away and spreading my legs wider.

His cock is hot and blunt at my entrance. His hips move in short strokes like a pendulum in and out of me, but he doesn't dare take me to the hilt. Again and again he swings in and out, and then I think I'm going to die if I don't feel him knocking the back of my cervix.

"Julien, please, harder," I say, not recognizing the sound of my own voice.

"Can't, Love. I'll hurt you."

If any other man said such words, I'd think him an arrogant idiot, but Julien's got the goods, and I'm about to bear the glorious brunt.

Thirty seconds later, Julien's thickness is butted up against the back wall of my sex, and he's holding my hips flush to his body like he doesn't want me to get away. I'm thankful we're in this position. "Go easy, please. It's been a long time for me."

Then he starts.

Slow at first, Julien gradually picks up speed, and it's just right. Before I know it, he's banging into me, nudging me up the table. He lowers my hips to the table and continues to thrust, holding himself upright with one hand. With the other, he presses his thumb against my clit again. The way he's stretching and filling me is a height of sensation I've never felt.

"Come with me, Amelia," he says, and I'm right there with him.

Our shouts and cries go on for what feels like minutes. When it's over, I pull him down and though sated, our kisses remain hungry until we're too tired to hold up our heads. We lay like that for some time, his body still inside mine and his ear to my chest, while I brush the damp hair from his forehead.

"There's a shower in that washroom," he says. "We should get ourselves cleaned up, and then I'll take you home."

I smile as we right ourselves, because today three dreams have come true. I've landed my first movie deal, Julien and I have had sex, and I will be working for Christine instead of Julien.

He stands by the door to the washroom, smiling, his hand outstretched for me. I attempt to close the leather corset around me and laugh at the lost cause.

I grab for my purse — lipstick and makeup for after the shower — and hear my phone ringing. I hope it's Chloe because I can't wait to tell her the good news. I raise my index finger to Julien. I don't recognize the number, but it's likely Chloe calling from the hospital.

I pick up. "Great news, Chlo!"

"Well, my little prodigy," Derek says. "I'm certainly eager to hear about this good news."

COMING
DECEMBER 2015

the corset maker

Volume Two

Thank you for reading THE CORSET MAKER, Volume One. This story about Amelia and Julien unfolds over a series of novellas.

To ensure you don't miss details about upcoming releases, be sure to subscribe to K.T.'s author newsletter at http://ktfrederick.com/vip-readers.